A Chance to Be

JS WILLIAMS

JS WILLIAMS, LLC

Contents

Dedication

To my two boys, who have been patient with their mom while she has become a writer in addition to her full time job as well as being a mother.

Acknowledgement

I want to acknowledge the people in my life who may find themselves or a reference they recognize in this book. I may or may have mentioned this to them. How does that meme go? "Be Careful Or You'll End Up In My Book."

Chapter I

HENRY

I've snorkeled in some of the most beautiful spots in the world. And the Bay of Palma counted as one of them. The warm waters were soothing as I swam along, looking at the sandy bottom. I watched the bream and wrasse drift along on the underwater current, in envy of their ability to float along with no care.

In the beautiful waters off the coast of the island of Mallorca, on vacation, I was enjoying some time alone. The harbor, filled with superyachts, and the area were famous for its beaches and the busy summer tourist season. Since I was far away from the hotel and resort swimming area, I never expected to be bumped into from behind.

I shot to the surface, ready to curse out whoever had interrupted my swim. Breaking through the seawater at the same time as the other person, I faced auburn hair being swept away by an arm as a woman removed her snorkel from her mouth. I saw clear blue eyes and a shocked look behind the snorkel mask as the woman apologized immediately.

"I am so sorry! I wasn't looking where I was going, and this was all my fault. Wait, do you speak English? I mean...*Hablas inglés*?" The woman questioned.

She reached behind her and smoothed her hair back more, feeling the back of her head. "Dang it, my hair tie broke. It's all snarled in my hair. I give up," she said as she took off her snorkel mask and continued to tread water.

I responded with surprise, "*Si, hablo inglés*. Yes, I speak English."

"You're an American!" The woman said, filled with excitement and amazement. "This is going to make things much simpler. I can speak Spanish, but not well." She laughed as she explained and then rubbed at her eyes where the saltwater had dribbled down from her hand. I swiped at my face, realizing it was dripping.

"My name's Evy Braam." She held out her hand as she tread water.

I shook her hand. Both were cold and wrinkled from swimming in the cool ocean water. "Henry. Nice to meet you; apology accepted. Are you from one of the other boats?" I wondered, looking in all directions.

"I'm staying at a resort close to here, and I'm quite a bit from the swimming area." Evy answered sheepishly.

Chuckling, I asked, "Just a bit?"

"I assume you're from one of these boats?" Evy asked, clearly impressed.

Suddenly, I realized that with the snorkel, goggles, and swim cap on, Evy couldn't tell who I was. I was used to everyone knowing who I was everywhere I went. Anonymity was something I hadn't experienced in a very long time. If I wanted to go out in public and avoid the paparazzi, I wore a hat and sometimes sunglasses, but this was different. Perhaps I should...could try a regular life for a bit, even just briefly.

I gestured vaguely with my left hand towards the west. "That boat brought me here to snorkel. I'm also staying at a resort, but haven't checked in yet. I did this first."

"You just got here? Me too! I arrived today and came directly to the beach after I got here." Evy grinned when she told me this. I realized when she smiled how her face lit up. She seemed so genuine and full of life, not artificial and full of herself like so many of the people I dealt with regularly.

Maybe I should take this chance. It's been a while since I truly connected with anyone, let alone a woman. Evy was beautiful, and I was enjoying talking to her, even for this short time.

"As much as I'm enjoying this conversation, I'm tired of treading water." I stated. "Perhaps our paths will cross; Magaluf isn't huge."

Evy responded, "That would be wonderful! Maybe I'll see you later!" Then she put on her snorkeling mask and took off toward the swimming area. As she did so, her fins lightly splashed me; the small droplets stung my eyes and flashed in the sunlight.

Placing my snorkel in my mouth, I swam back towards my yacht. I climbed onto it from the back and then glanced behind me, checking to make sure Evy didn't see me get on it. I accepted the gray towel from my personal assistant, Erik, and dried off. As Erik turned away, I called him back.

"Erik, get me a pair of binoculars, quick," I instructed.

Surprised, Erik glanced at me and then rushed inside the yacht to grab the binoculars from where they were in a cabinet. He brought them out and handed them over. "Here you go. But what exactly are you looking for?"

Ignoring the other man, I turned towards the beach and peered through the lenses. Spotting a mass of auburn hair exiting the water, I adjusted the clarity so I could make out if it was the woman, Evy, that I'd just been talking to. It was!

I continued observing as she walked to a towel, picked it up to dry herself off, and collected her other items on the beach. She then walked across the sand to a set of stairs that led to a road.

"Damn!" I exclaimed out loud, thinking I was going to lose sight of her.

"What is going on?" asked Erik.

Waving a hand at my assistant to be quiet, I never took my eyes from the binoculars. Evy had reached the top of the stairs, and I wanted to see which way she went. The idea of never seeing her again made my chest tighten. Instead of questioning the feeling, I watched as she didn't turn but crossed the road, then entered the resort on the other side of the street from the stairs. I couldn't see the name, but that didn't matter. I now knew that I had the chance to see her again.

Taking the binoculars down, I held them in my hands and turned to my assistant. "I want you to find out the name of the resort that is across from those stairs," I pointed toward the beach. "Then book me the best room at that resort for the next week."

Erik looked at me in shock. "What? Why?"

"Just do it," I interjected. I walked from the back of the yacht to the bar to grab a glass bottle of cold water. As I twisted off the top and took a gulp of the refreshingly cool liquid, I didn't glance at Erik, knowing that there would be a questioning look on his face. Even though Erik was three years younger than I was, the man acted like my senior sometimes. Truthfully, more often than not.

"I have been with you for six years. This is a side of you I've never seen, Henry," Erik's grumbling was an obvious sign of my assistant's feelings.

Setting the bottle down on the wooden bar, I circled back to Erik. "I'm telling you this in confidence. As my personal assistant and my friend. I just met a woman who didn't know who I was and talked to me like a normal person. There was also a connection there that I've never had with any other woman. I'd just like to explore it like anyone else. You know how difficult and rare that is for me."

Erik's eyes widened at this. A smile slowly spread across his face, and the stony look he had before melted away. "I'll begin working on it right away. It may take me a few hours, though."

"That sounds good because I have another fa-vor. I need to keep my identity a secret. It shouldn't be too hard since I usually wear those colored contacts for my role as Vigil Warden. If I cut my hair short, it'll look different from the longer style I normally wear. How do you feel about helping me cut my hair?"

The assistant turned back to look at me with a raised eyebrow. "Okay? You're going to trust me to cut your hair?"

Nodding, I looked directly into Erik's eyes in gratitude. "Thank you. For all your help. I simply want a chance to be me."

EVY

I looked in the mirror. The lightweight, flowy, navy blue sundress with a milkmaid neckline and corset back was more than I probably needed for dinner, but I'd felt like dressing up. I loved the way it brushed against my skin. A tingle went up my spine, then down again, as the fabric floated around my legs.

As a mother of two in my late twenties, I didn't get the chance to dress up often. I rarely wore makeup or heels either. Running around after two young children usually meant I didn't need to wear them. Today I wore both. My makeup was minimal but classy: blush on my cheeks, shimmery multicolor eyeshadow, and lip stain with a gloss over it. The gloss had a slight pink tint and a strawberry flavor. It had been a splurge when I'd bought it. My other splurge had been a travel-size perfume, which I spritzed on my wrists and at the base of my throat.

I was in Mallorca, Spain, for the next week on vacation! It was like a dream come true. I'd read that this was one of Europe's prime vacation spots. For me, it had been one of the cheaper places to go when I'd looked at booking a trip. Advertisements described the place as having some of the most beautiful beaches, historical sites to visit, and many local restaurants. Even though I was by myself rather than with someone, which would have been more fun, I'd still enjoy this trip.

Spinning to survey my resort room, I had to pinch myself. The resort and room could be mistaken for one in the US until you looked closer. My room had a balcony that looked out over the family pool, and I'd already seen one woman at it with her top off. That had been an initial shock to my American self, but I'd quickly pushed my prudishness aside. The major difference between this resort and American ones, as far as I could tell, was that air conditioning was only in the guest rooms. The public and dining areas were mostly open to the outside. It had taken me a bit to figure out how to set the air conditioner to the right temperature in Celsius. I laughed, remembering how I'd had to use my phone to look up the conversion.

I took one last look in the mirror, tucked a strand of my shoulder-length auburn hair behind my ear as I'd left it in waves to frame my face tonight, and slipped my feet into a pair of wedge sandals. Swiveling, I grabbed my phone and left the room. The evening humidity immediately struck me, threatening to curl and frizz my hair. I tucked my key card into the wallet that was attached to the back of my phone, thankful I had it to carry that in as I headed to the elevator. It made it so that I didn't have to carry a purse around the resort. I'd decided to eat in the à la carte restaurant area tonight.

The elevator opened on the main floor, and I followed the signs that pointed the way out of the lobby towards the food court. I took a step outside, listening to the automatic doors swoosh shut behind me. The setting sun momentarily blinded me, so I put my hand up to shield my eyes and then waited for them to acclimate as I took a couple of steps forward past the doors. As I took my hand from my eyes, I thought I heard my name, though I was sure I had to be mistaken.

"Evy, is that you?" A voice spoke near me.

Looking around, I saw a man in his mid-thirties getting up from a chair on the side of the prom-enade walkway, who must've been the one talk-ing. He was a few inches over six feet tall, with a medium build, black hair that was cut short on top with a faded shave on the sides, and green eyes. It took me a second to place the voice.

"Um, Henry?" I inquired.

"Yes! What a coincidence! You're also staying at this resort?" Henry asked as he moved beside me. The top of my head came to just over his shoulder.

I responded, "That's right. You too, I take it?"

"Of course. It looks like you're heading to din-ner. Please don't let me keep you from whoever you're with."

I answered, "I'm traveling and eating solo. There is no one waiting for me."

Henry responded, "Me too. Mind if I join you?"

"Sure! I was going to try the à la carte restau-rants here at the resort."

Henry replied, "I hadn't decided, so that sounds good."

Henry held out his arm to me, and I took it. Together we walked the length of the promenade to the stairs that led to the next floor down, where the food court was located.

Flowering plants and greenery lined the way to the stairs, which made the air smell of orchids and rosemary. I'd thought that Henry was handsome when we were out in the water, but seeing him now, I saw he was better looking than I'd originally thought. His bright green eyes were what I liked most. They reminded me of young spring tree buds just before they burst into leaves. And his gaze was direct and unwavering—a sure sign of confidence.

The two of us browsed the options available at the four different stations before deciding on our dinner choices, filling our plates, and then picking out seats. When Henry leaned close to point out options to me, I picked up on his cologne. It reminded me of a combination of the ocean and woods: sea salt and cypress.

At the table, Henry held the chair out for me. Once seated, a waiter came to take our drink orders.

"I'd like to try a locally made wine. What do you have in a white wine, preferably on the sweet side?" I requested. I didn't drink wine very often, but wanted to try something new tonight.

The waiter replied. "Of course, *senorita*. I have a wine in mind just for you. For you, *senor*?"

Henry responded, *"Cerveza, por favor."*

"Cómo lo quieres?" asked the waiter.

Answering in fluent Spanish, Henry answered the waiter. *"Frío, por favor. Y gracias."*

The waiter brought me a Spanish *Màlaga*. It ended up being one of the best wines I'd ever had, with notes of raisin and citrus. I noticed Henry had his beer cold, the American way.

The food also did not disappoint. I'd gone with the *sobrasada* with honey, a *tagliatelle* entrée, and *tiramisu* for dessert. I'd picked my choices by going with things I'd never had before or that I was craving. Meanwhile, Henry had chosen the *pancetta* penne with a side of bread and skipped dessert. I'd noticed that he seemed familiar with most of the food options.

I leaned forward and asked, "Okay, tell me where the name Henry came from. I have to admit I've been curious about it since you first told me about it. It's pretty old-fashioned, though that's the style for a baby now." We were now sipping after-dinner drinks. I had chosen a port, and he had a glass of whiskey.

Laughing, Henry set down his drink and crossed his arms on the table. "My father and I share the same first name but have different middle names, so we've always been called by those. His middle name is John, and mine is Henry. I think it started when I was born, but I've been called Henry for as long as I can remember."

I responded, "That's actually interesting. Few people now share a name with a parent."

"Now tell me something about yourself that's just as interesting," he requested.

Tapping my cheek with one finger, I thought for a moment. "How about this? I'm Dutch on my father's side and mostly Irish on my mom's.

She's who I got my red hair from. My name means 'life' or 'breathe' and is Dutch."

"That is quite an interesting combination. You've gotten me intrigued. Tell me more about yourself." Henry placed his head on one hand, his elbow on the table. He was clearly ready to listen to my life story.

Sitting back in the seat with my port, I cupped the glass while I talked. "I was born and raised in a small town in western Michigan. My mom and aunt, who share a house, live next door to me. Since my mom is semi-retired and her sister is fully retired, they are watching my two children from a previous marriage. My best friend is also helping while I'm gone. I'm so lucky to have such support and help. My dad passed away when I was a teenager, so it was just my mom and me for quite a while."

"And what do you do for a living?" Henry inquired.

"I'm a certified teacher. I teach preschoolers at a daycare," I answered.

Henry whistled. "You have way more patience than I would."

A smile crossed my face. "I love my job. In fact, I actually already miss my children and the kids at the daycare." I paused and looked at him. "Now it's your turn."

Situating himself in his chair, Henry paused before talking, "I live in New York City, and I'm an actor. Though I grew up in North Dakota, where my parents and brother still live."

"An actor? How did you become interested in acting?" I asked.

Henry blushed a little at that, "That was a middle school mistake. I stumbled upon drama by putting it down as an elective to fill a spot on the class sheet. It had not been a course I had meant to take, but ended up with it and fell in love with it. That teacher became one of my favorites and a mentor. From the second semester of seventh grade on, I took drama or was involved in any form of theater that I could."

"How did your parents take the news that you loved acting? Some parents wouldn't find that worthwhile."

"I was fortunate that my parents supported my love of acting. Later, I moved to New York City to attend acting school and pursue my dream of being an actor. Obviously, that's where I stayed after I graduated."

We talked about our likes and dislikes, and I was stunned at how much we had in common. It turned out that we both enjoyed musicals and reading, and preferred to spend nights in over going to clubs or bars.

The night wore on as we revealed more details and learned about each other. It became so late that the waiter came to tell us that the food court was closed, but we could move to any of the bars. Amazed, we exchanged glances, not having marked the time nor the temperature difference as the evening had progressed. We reluctantly said goodnight instead of going to a bar.

As I entered my room, I thought about how much I had revealed to this virtual stranger. Henry had offered to walk me back to my room because of the late hour, and I'd accepted. I tossed a glance back out the door, then swung my head back around when I saw Henry had stopped at the stairway to look back at me. This connection I felt with him, I'd never come close to feeling with my ex-husband. And it scared me.

Chapter 2

HENRY

The next morning, the buzz of the phone woke me up. It was a text notification from Erik. He wanted to know if the room was to my satisfaction, since the resort wasn't my 'usual' and if I wanted to come back to the yacht. I swiped to mute the notification and flipped over, grinning from ear to ear as I remembered the evening before. I couldn't recall when I'd spent time in such a relaxing way, just talking with someone. No pretense, no preening, and not having to worry about ratings.

I loved the sparkle in her blue eyes when she talked about the people in her life, and swore I could lose myself in their depths. When I'd left, I'd wondered, *Would Evy want to see me again tomorrow? Had she enjoyed our time together as much as I had? How could I finagle that?* Evy was down to earth and exactly what I expected. She was the woman I'd always hoped to find. Now, all I had to do was figure out how to keep her.

How could she fit into my world?

Of course, first I had to tell her who I really am. The smile fell away from my face with this thought. I wasn't sure that I was ready to do that yet. She thought I was just a normal guy, not a world-famous movie star.

Hopping out of bed, I prepared to start the day and hoped I could spend more time with Evy. I wanted to believe that she would feel the same after our evening. I also wondered if she'd wear the perfume she'd on last night again. It smelled of black pepper, lavender, and patchouli. I'd never thought that I would like that combination, but on Evy it was intoxicating.

Sprinting through my shower, I got dressed as quickly as I could. Putting on a pair of cargo shorts, a graphic t-shirt, and sandals, I grabbed a hat and was ready to leave the room before remembering a pair of sunglasses. Glimpsing my reflection in the mirror, I was amazed at how one little thing had changed my appearance so much. The haircut had changed my profile so that even I didn't quite recognize myself.

I walked through the courtyard to the pathway that separated the building where my room was from the main one. Old cobblestones made up the pathway, and some of them were uneven. As I neared the family pool outside the building where Evy's room was, I wondered if she was awake yet. The sun was just up in the sky, warming the new day and bringing in the humidity. I knew which room was Evy's, as I'd walked her back last night with it having been so late.

As I walked into the family pool area, I glanced towards where I knew her room was, and saw her on her balcony, already dressed in white shorts and an abstract-patterned tank top. A ponytail held her hair up. Our eyes locked. She smiled at me, and I smiled back.

I called out to her, waving, "Have you eaten?"

Evy shook her head. "I'll meet you downstairs in the lobby."

Giving her a thumbs-up, I headed into the building. Inside, I walked up to the lobby desk and asked where the closest local bakery was. I'd just finished getting the directions as Evy stepped out of the elevator. I walked up to meet her and, without thinking, leaned down to peck her on the cheek. Evy gasped and put a hand to the place on her face where my lips had been.

I stepped back, shocked at what I'd done, and apologized. "Evy, I'm sorry. I don't know what came over me."

I watched a blush spread across her cheeks as she hesitated and then stammered. "No, it's all right. I was just surprised."

"I have directions to a local bakery; perhaps we could go there," I said quickly to deflect, and glanced away to the door. "We can walk to it."

Lifting a hand, she touched my face, gazed at me, and then stated, "That sounds lovely."

Bringing her hand down, Evy reached out and took my hand in hers timidly. I responded by beaming at her and gripping her hand. Evy smiled back at me as we walked out of the resort. The walk to the bakery took about ten minutes, and we spent it quietly, enjoying the time together.

Around us, Malaga was busy with people walking at their own pace, cars driving by, and birds flying overhead. We had to let go of each other's hands when we neared a bus stop full of people waiting for the TIB line. The public transportation system seemed to be a popular way to get around on the island of Mallorca. Once past, I reached for Evy's hand so I could clasp it again. The feel of her hand in mine was calming.

The way the sunlight hit Evy's auburn hair entranced me, changing it from a bronzed red to a deep mahogany. I wanted to run my hands through it. I could only imagine how soft it felt.

Arriving at the bakery, we took seats, ordered coffee and a couple of different *ensaïmada*, the spiral cakes that are local to Mallorca, which we shared. The cakes were buttery and melted in our mouths. Evy laughed when I reached across the table to brush crumbs and apricot from her cheek with a napkin.

As we drank our coffee, I reached across the table and held Evy's hand. Staring into her eyes, I figured I needed to confess and apologize. "Kissing you this morning felt like the most natural thing to do. I can't put it any other way; I know we just met yesterday, but it seems like I've known you forever. I want to see where this goes. What are your plans for today? Can we spend the rest of the day together?" I begged, placing my hand on her cheek.

Evy leaned slightly into my hand. "I would like that. If I were to describe fate, I would say that's what this is. So, we should see it through. Last night we talked about what sights we would want to see. Should we do that?"

We finished the rest of the pastries and coffee as we planned out the day of sightseeing together. I pulled up a website with the main sights of the island that offered a tour. I kept one of her hands in mine, trying to swipe my phone with just one hand. There was a need in me not to lose connection with Evy.

"We can take this tour that has stops and audio to listen to. Each stop is optional, and it comes with tickets to get into two of the sights, specifically the castle and cathedral." I read the description out loud to Evy.

"That sounds perfect! I definitely want to visit both. The other area I want to go to is Old Town. Where did you want to visit?"

I looked at the list of stops on the phone again before answering. "I also wanted to see the castle and the cathedral. Old Town sounds interesting. I haven't really done much looking into that. The palace near the cathedral also requires a separate ticket. I see the bus goes near a museum and an art gallery. Those would definitely be neat to go to if we have time."

"Sounds like we kind of know what we want to do. Let's just wing the rest." Evy grinned and grabbed her purse from beside her as she stood up. She laughed when I refused to let go of her hand.

We headed back to the resort to gather what we wanted to take into town. After catching a taxi into *Palma de Mallorca*, we played tourist.

EVY

My favorite places to visit were the castle and Old Town. Walking around a fourteenth-century castle had been a dream, but a rare round one was cooler than the typical castle.

Standing atop Castell de Bellver, I said to Henry, "Look at the carvings made by former prisoners." I traced one with my finger. It showed the date 1909. A shiver ran up my spine, and goosebumps appeared on my arms.

Henry ran his hand up and down one of my arms to chase away the bumps. "Makes you wonder what the person was doing up here on top of the castle when it was a prison. Though the view up here is beautiful."

I turned to him to agree but discovered that he wasn't looking at the harbor on one side or the mountain on the other; he was watching me. I felt heat spreading up my chest to my neck and cheeks. Hurrying, I turned around and headed back down the stairs. I wasn't sure how to respond to his comment.

Our next stop was Old Town. Unique wooden doors filled the cobbled streets. I couldn't stop from taking photos of them. Wandering where others had been for hundreds of years and wondering what stories had unraveled there had been the focus of Henry's and my conversation while we walked.

"What is this?" I asked wonderingly at a building that sat in the fork of two streets. It was round with window-like openings that were covered with grating. I read the small sign on one side. "*Font del Sepulcre*. What does that mean?" I asked Henry.

Henry explained. "It means Fountain of the Tomb. Let me see what I can find about this place. I'll look it up," he said, waving his phone and then diving into his research.

"Wow, this is so interesting! They constructed the fountain in the 13th century over a cistern dating back to the 10th century. Behind the fountain is the rest of a church that was built over a mosque. The Christians wanted to change the entire area to Christian once they took it over from the Arabs." The excitement on Henry's face and in his voice was exactly how I felt. I continued to be amazed at how similar we were.

We resumed walking through Old Town hand in hand, soon arriving at the *Carrer del Palau Relel*, a major street with lots of restaurants and shops. We stopped and sat by one of the many fountains. This one was a column split at the base with four turtles that I absolutely adored. But then I tried to take a photo of it and almost fell in while doing so. I hadn't paid attention and walked too close to the edge, rather than using the camera zoom.

As I yelped, Henry called out. "Evy, watch out!"

I felt him grab me by the waist and quickly draw me back, which made me catch my breath both from the unexpectedness of it and the shock of being held against his body. I also dropped my phone, but was later glad I had put it on a wrist strap so it didn't fall to the ground. Henry was slow to release me, and I felt his hands slide away instead of just letting go.

"Thank you," I breathed as I brushed my hair away from my face, patting my clothes back into place, and then taking a step away. As I did, my stomach growled, and I made a face as Henry laughed at me.

"Let's find a place to eat so your stomach stops talking."

I hit him on the arm, which caused him to laugh at me again.

We walked further down the street and ate at an outdoor cafe near the cathedral and the palace. Pub fare in Spain turned out to be very similar to the food served in the US.

The lack of tax and tips in Europe kept me surprised. It was so ingrained in Americans that I kept trying to include it when I paid, including the bill at the cafe.

"Let's see. The total is 23.45 euros." I read from the bill.

Henry handed me some money for his portion. I added my money to his and then set another bill to the side that he didn't notice. When the server came over, she took the money, thanked us, and left. I got up to leave, and Henry picked up the other bill to hand back to me.

I frowned at Henry. "That is the server's tip! Leave it on the table."

Henry chuckled at me. "The server won't take your money, or she will give it back to you. They don't take tips here."

"Ugh. I keep forgetting!" I admitted.

At the cathedral, we discovered we'd missed the time to tour it. There were apparently limited opening hours. Our tickets were valid for any day, though, so we could come back another day. Instead, we walked along the outside, admiring the architecture and the promenade that overlooked the *Parc de la Mar*, which had a beautiful fountain in the middle.

"Can you imagine what this looks like at night?" I pondered as I leaned against the wall, looking out over the water next to the *Catedral-Basílica de Santa María de Mallorca*.

I glanced at Henry to find him watching me again. He had been doing this a lot during our day out.

"I imagine it looks absolutely stunning," Henry replied. I blushed, realizing he wasn't talking about the surrounding scenery.

The palace that Henry had mentioned was right across from the cathedral, so we bought tickets and toured that instead. The Royal Palace of *La Almudaina*, like many other historical sites, had been Arabic before its transition in the 12th century.

As we walked through it, I was in awe of the palace. "I can't believe the artistry of the building, the rugs, just everything. I could stay forever in the gardens alone."

Equally wonder-struck, Henry was filling his phone with photos. Later, I'd discover that he was not just capturing the sights of the palace, but also me and my reaction to everything we saw.

HENRY

It endeared Evy to me even more to have seen her in such real-life situations. Whenever I'd been in Mallorca before, I'd kept to myself on the yacht. It had been too much work to hide my identity just to go into town and risk being seen.

I was actually a very laid-back person, and when I'd become a world-renowned celebrity, I hadn't realized how much of my privacy I'd give up. However, I enjoyed spending time with Evy, and I believed the risk of recognition was worth it.

We arrived back at the resort late, so had dinner at a nearby restaurant inside another resort. It opened onto the bay, and the breeze that blew in kept the humidity down and the temperature comfortable.

"I have to admit that I've fallen in love with Mallorca. It's so peaceful here. In a way, it reminds me of the feeling when I sit by a lake in Michigan," Evy confessed.

I peered at her over the hand I held up, since the sun was setting over the Mediterranean Sea and shining in my face. "Really? I've never been to Michigan. Tell me what that's like. I've been to the Atlantic Ocean and the Pacific Ocean, but not a Great Lake. We didn't have any lakes near us growing up in North Dakota, only rivers."

"I usually go to the lake near town, not Lake Michigan. That's just over an hour away. Big Pine Island Lake has a boat ramp, and I like to go sit at it just to stare out over the water. I've taken my children to Lake Michigan once. They're still too young to swim there a lot yet. A great lake is a lot like an ocean or sea. It has current and large waves. They put out flags to show what the level is for swimming, just like they do here," Evy answered him.

"We also have a major river that runs through town, the Flat River, and I'll go sit by that too. It's just as peaceful. There is a specific spot I've found that few people go to so I can be by myself."

I grinned at the dreamy quality that had come over Evy's face as she talked about her hometown and state. It had been a long time since I'd been to Hillsboro for more than a quick visit. I honestly missed being in a small town.

The waitress arrived at that moment to take our order. We'd already picked water to drink and had each chosen not to have any other drinks since it was so late. We decided to share a seafood paella. Evy had never had it before, and since it was a dish to share, I had it with her.

When it arrived, Evy bubbled with excitement over its size. The paella dish was as large as a pizza pan and set on the table on a stand.

"I've never seen a pan so large in my life except for one for pizza!" She gushed. "It smells divine! I hope it tastes just as wonderful."

I served us both the Spanish dish of saffron-infused rice mixed with vegetables, chorizo, shrimp, chicken, mussels, and clams. I made sure to serve up the crispy rice at the bottom of the dish called the *socarrat*.

Holding up the fork with the succulent dish on it, I fed a bite to her. I watched as Evy's eyes widened in delight at her first taste. She put a hand to her mouth. "Wow, just wow. I've never tasted anything like this!"

Smiling, I took a bite. "I'm glad you like it. I've had it before, but having it with someone who never has makes me appreciate it even more."

We finished dinner, and I paid the bill despite Evy's protests. When I left Evy at her doorway, I leaned down to kiss her, which she met halfway.

That did something to me. I hadn't been sure if she'd let me or pull back at the last second, but she leaned in like she wanted it just as much. The hesitation I'd been holding onto disappeared the second her lips touched mine.

The kiss lingered, longer than it should have for a first one. Soft at first, then just a little deeper, like neither of us was quite ready to let go. Her lips were warm, and when she pressed closer, I felt it straight through my chest. My hand settled at her waist before I could stop myself, pulling her in just enough to feel the curve of her against me.

For a second, I forgot where we were. Forgot the door at her back, forgot everything except the way she felt in my arms and the quiet, steady way she kissed me back like she meant it.

I pulled away slowly, not because I wanted to, but because I knew if I didn't, I might not stop there. And that stayed with me long after I stepped back.

Afterwards, I didn't let go right away, and she didn't pull away. The air between us shifted, heavier, as if one more second would change everything. I wanted to keep going. Hell, I knew she did too. But neither of us crossed that line.

Chapter 3

Evy

T he next morning, while getting ready to meet Henry, I thought about the day before. I had thoroughly enjoyed playing tourist and spending time with him. Then I recalled when he'd brushed crumbs from my mouth. I'd wondered what I looked like then, probably a mess. But his touch had sent a frisson of sparks through me that had cut my laughter short.

...and that KISS...While it had surprised me, it had not felt...wrong. In fact, it had felt natural. Almost too natural. As did everything about Henry and me together.

I contemplated how me and Henry had shared our growing feelings for each other. My relationship with Vincent, the twins' father, had lasted for almost eight years. I had met him at the end of high school; we had dated for over three years, then been married for close to four years before divorcing.

My pregnancy had been the main reason for our breakup. We had already been having issues in our relationship right before finding out about the twins. Vincent had never wanted children, so when we found out I was pregnant, and then discovered it was multiples, that was the last straw for him. He had accused me of manipulating him by getting pregnant even though he had never wanted me to be on birth control and insisted on condoms for preventing pregnancy, knowing they weren't foolproof.

I recalled one of our arguments.

"You're pregnant?" Vincent had said in an accusatory tone.

I had hoped that he would be happy, even though he had previously expressed that he didn't want children. But this was our child.

"Aren't you happy, even a little?" I had asked him.

Vincent had started to pace our living room but stopped at my question and glared at me. "No! I told you I didn't want kids. Now you went and got pregnant." He had then stormed out of the house.

I'd felt tears gather upon hearing the blame in his voice. As if I had done this to trap him instead of this being a blessing. I'd mistakenly thought that this pregnancy would be a way to fix our marriage. Instead, it would ultimately be the end.

I would spend the entire pregnancy alone, even giving birth to the twins. During that time, I beat myself up, wondering if there had been a way to save the marriage to Vincent if I had not become pregnant. I knew now that would never have happened. There had been too many differences between us, and we would've grown apart no matter what.

Now, here I was jumping into love with someone I had literally just met. This wasn't me, but as I had told Henry, it was like stepping into a moment that was meant to be. Like fate had quietly guided us here. Things were happening too easily, and we got along so well. The next question was, how far was I willing to let things go?

Once ready, I met Henry as agreed, early, to spend the day together again. We'd discussed the previous day continuing our tourism by visiting *Port de Soller* and then returning to find another local place to have dinner in Magaluf, but one that had more traditional food options. "Good morning!" called Henry from outside the resort. He waved from where he was waiting for me. We had agreed to have breakfast before we left.

Smiling, I walked over to meet him. I took his hand and gave him a peck on the cheek. I had decided that I would enjoy this time together.

We took the taxi once again into *Palma de Mallorca*, this time to take the train to Soller. It was from 1912 and remodeled to its glory. However, that meant that there was no air conditioning, nor even a fan in the train car. The only break from the heat was when the train went through the tunnels carved into the mountains. The train car went dark, and the air became dirty-smelling and damp. This would have been extremely interesting for me, except that I ended up sitting on Henry's lap for the trip because of the lack of seating. The packed train made what we had thought would be a romantic journey a little less appealing than it originally sounded.

"Follow me. Let's find some seats." Henry had taken the lead, pulling me by the hand to the front of the train, using his height to look through the windows into the train cars.

He had led me up the stairs of one, stating, "This one looks promising."

I'd followed, and we had sat side by side on a bench. We'd read the brochure we had picked up at the station while waiting for the ride to start. Soon, there had been an announcement.

"We have a full train today. Some passengers will need to stand."

Henry had peered at me as more people crowded into the train car. I stood up as an older woman entered, offering her the seat I had just vacated. Henry stood as well to give the woman's husband his seat. That left a single chair for both of us.

Raising an eyebrow, Henry had gestured to it.

I'd protested, "No, you sit. I'll take the armrest."

He had then glowered at me. "There is no way I am sitting in the chair."

"Why don't we share it then?" I had offered the compromise. "I can sit on your lap, I mean leg."

A look of surprise crossed Henry's face before he understood what I meant. Finally, he jerked his head in a single nod of agreement and sat just as the train pulled out of the station.

I had tried to sit on just one leg, but with the jostling of the train, I'd soon fell full onto his lap. As each turn of the train made me shift, I could feel the ridge of Henry's growing hardness under me. I could only imagine it was as agonizing for him as it was for me. After a short while, I gasped when Henry's arm snaked around me, low around my waist, to grasp my opposite hip, holding me in place.

"Don't move," He hissed between clenched teeth.

His other arm gripped the armrest. I saw him looking toward the window, though he had his eyes shut and his jaw tensed. I realized it was taking his entire concentration to maintain his control.

I swallowed and stilled my body. "Sorry," I whispered.

As soon as the train stopped for the break at *Pujol d'en Banya*, I leapt up and left the train to walk around outside. I placed the small backpack I'd brought on his lap as I left to give him privacy and time to deal with the situation.

"I'll, um, be back soon," I stammered.

Outside, I walked around, rubbing my arms, trying to calm down. My body felt like it was on fire, and my breathing was ragged. The sexual connection between Henry and me was undeniable. By the time the break at the viewing spot was over, I was more in control but definitely not back to normal.

Upon going back to the train, I stood next to the seat and leaned on the armrest, rather than endure that torture again. I couldn't meet his eyes for the entire rest of the trip, nor as we left the train. I noticed Henry couldn't either.

Once in Soller, we did not touch and, with an unspoken agreement, headed straight for the tram. It would take us to the port and also give us more time to calm down.

On it, Henry and I sat next to each other, and halfway through the ride, our hands found each other on the bench, weaving our fingers together. We looked at each other, a silent moment full of apology yet peace passing between us with only a smile.

After a moment, though, I giggled as I recalled the situation. I hurried and covered my mouth, then glanced at Henry in mortification. His own lips were quivering with laughter, and we both burst into chuckles as we bent over, fully laughing. People near us glanced our way, probably wondering about the crazy Americans.

After this release, we sat back and enjoyed the tram ride, commenting on the beauty and sights we saw on the way to the port.

"Oh my gosh, look how close we are to people eating at this place!" I exclaimed.

Henry was just as surprised as I. "I would be afraid to eat somewhere a train runs within a couple of feet of it."

"I think I can reach out and pull a lemon from that tree in that backyard." A laugh escaped Henry with his words.

Another sight that shocked me was when a person stepped right in front of the tram, despite its horn sounding. "I can't believe that person just walked in front of the tram! I would be terrified!"

"People here are probably used to it. I think I read that the trams run every hour from February to November. They're not just for tourists but also for the locals."

In the port town, we found a place for an early lunch. The camaraderie we had previously shared returned by then, and we laughed as we told stories from our childhood.

"Then I jumped off the roof of the barn with the umbrella, thinking it could hold my weight and I could fly just like Mary Poppins! My brother did too. My mom was so mad when she discovered we'd wrecked every single umbrella we owned." We were both laughing until we were out of breath listening to Henry tell his story. The picture he described of his brother and him trying to float using umbrellas off a barn roof was just too much.

I wiped away a tear, "I can't believe neither of you two broke a bone!"

"I can't believe it either. We definitely were two hellions. That my mom is sane after raising us is probably a miracle." He chuckled at this and then paid the bill for our food.

After eating, our walk around was full of ducking in and out of little shops while continuing to hold hands. I couldn't get enough of his touch. I figured he thought the same as I caught him rubbing his thumb across the back of my hand more than once.

I stopped at one shop and stared through the window at the jewelry. It specialized in saltwater pearls. I suddenly felt a yank on my arm.

"Wha..!?" I yelped as Henry pulled me into the store.

The next thing I knew, Henry insisted on buying me a black pearl necklace with matching earrings. The set was beautiful, but I thought it was too much money for him to spend.

"Henry, I can't accept this! It's way too much money."

Henry was already paying for the jewelry while I was still protesting. "Nonsense. Plus, they look too good on you to leave them sitting here in a store gathering dust."

The salesperson looked on with delight and fondness. She knew she had made a great sale, but she also listened to our bickering, knowing that Henry would win.

Huffing, I gave in and took the bag. "This means the next treat is on me, though."

When we came across the famous Soller ice cream, I insisted on him letting me buy it. Oranges from the island were used to make the frozen custard. It was delicious, and we both giggled when my ice cream melted down my hand. Henry brought my hand to his mouth and licked the sweet mess clean. I shivered both from the cold cream and from the touch of his tongue. He stared at me with hooded eyes as I held my breath when he did this. His look seemed to ask a question I wasn't sure I was ready to answer.

After touring the port, we took the tram back to Soller, where we toured a 17th-century cathedral as well as walked through the streets of the town. A rose window that overlooked the main entrance dominated the *Església de Sant Bartomeu*. Fourteen small inset chapels graced the interior. At the one called the 'Chapel of Souls,' I paid a euro to light a candle in memory of my father.

Henry stood to one side as I whispered a prayer. "Lord, I light this candle in loving memory of my father. Grant him eternal rest, and let Your perpetual light shine upon him. Hold him in Your mercy and peace until we meet again. Amen."

Since the cathedral was only a couple of blocks away from *la estacion de tren*, we headed there next, then it was back on the train to *Palma de Mallorca*. This time the train wasn't even close to full, so we could sit side by side and enjoy the trip. Because it was less crowded, we also enjoyed talking and the scenery, including going through the tunnels.

I shared tidbits about my children, Matthew and Cora, who were three-year-old twins. I told him how I missed them, but was also glad for some time away. My ex-husband wasn't an involved father and said that the children had been part of the reason for our breakup. I was really like a single parent to them most of the time.

"I'm so sorry that your ex doesn't help," Henry agonized with me.

I shrugged my shoulders. "It's all right. I've been raising them now for almost four years by myself. It helps that they're such great kids." I smiled as I thought about my twins.

"Can I see a picture of them?" he asked. "I assume you have one."

Beaming, I pulled out my phone. "Of course I do!" I pulled up the photo app and a picture I'd taken right before I'd left. Twisting in the train seat, I handed the phone to Henry and watched as he grinned at the two children's pictures on my screen.

"I can see you in both of them," he assured me.

I confirmed. "They have my ex-husband's hair, but they definitely have my facial features."

Henry returned my phone and put his arms around my shoulders, pulling me close for the rest of the ride back to the station. I gave in and leaned my head on his shoulder. While not that late, we had done a lot of walking, and I was tired.

HENRY

Once back in *Palma de Mallorca*, we took a taxi back to the resort so we could shower and change before dinner. I'd found an upscale restaurant close to the resort, known for its traditional seafood entrees.

I was lounging in a wingback chair, waiting in the lobby when Evy stepped off the elevator. Evy said my name, and I heard her steps coming towards me, so I rose out of the chair and turned to walk towards her. The sight of her caused me to stop mid-step. She was wearing a black dress with cutouts that showed multi-colored fabric underneath, with zipper accents at the hem and shoulder. Her hair fell in waves to her shoulders. She had on the pearl necklace and earrings I'd bought her as well.

Evy was admiring me as much as I was admiring her. I was wearing a navy blue casual linen suit with a black t-shirt, a black leather belt, and black leather slip-on shoes. It was both casual and stylish at the same time. It also matched Evy without meaning to.

Offering her my hand, I said. "I've got a taxi, sweetheart, though it's close. I didn't think we would want to talk tonight."

The endearment came out without thought and caught us both off guard. I looked embarrassed, and Evy's eyes widened, but then she smiled at it. This made me relax and grin back at her.

Evy nodded in agreement, and the two of us walked out to the taxi. The drive wasn't long, as I'd said, and we spent it in silence. Evy laid her head on my shoulder as we shared the back seat of the taxi, holding hands. I surreptitiously shifted in the seat when the scent of patchouli and pepper caught my attention, making the front of my pants tighten. I recalled smelling the perfume when Evy sat on my lap in the train car, with the sway causing her to move so temptingly on me. The scent would forever remind me of that moment.

This was the best of all the dinners we had. The restaurant was right on the bay, giving us a beautiful view of the waters where we had first met. I recommended Evy try the fish stew, a local delicacy, and she was happy that she had. The combination of spices and freshly caught fish was amazing. I had the grilled shrimp, and we shared a *crema catalan* for dessert. Evy had a Spanish sherry as an evening cocktail, while I finished with a coffee.

Although we had talked a lot during the day, we mostly remained silent in the evening. Instead, touches and glances filled the time. She lingered close when she didn't need to, her fingers brushing mine as if it wasn't an accident. As the evening drew to a close, I had a feeling she wanted the same thing I did.

Upon arrival back at the resort, I took both of Evy's hands in mine and then slid them up her arms to her face. Cupping her jaw, I posed the question that needed to be voiced. "Evy, will you come with me to my room?"

Evy took a deep breath, rested one of her hands on my cheek, and looked into my green eyes. "Yes."

Chapter 4

HENRY

We walked hand in hand through the resort and followed the path to the building that housed my room. The smell of the orchids was strong as we walked along the pathway. It was a beautiful night, and the family pool was lit from the bottom and sides. No one was sitting around it or at any of the patio tables. We followed the winding sidewalk to the next building, which housed the adults-only pool and where my room was. I swiped my keycard to unlock the gate and held it for Evy. It squeaked lightly as it opened and then closed behind us.

I knew I had to tell Evy the truth about myself before we took our relationship to the next level. I hoped she wouldn't be upset at my deception and would understand why I'd hidden my identity. However, I knew it had to be done, and if she was too angry about my news, then I would have to let her go.

Since becoming an A-list actor, I hadn't had a successful relationship and tried dating actresses or models familiar with my lifestyle, but found most shallow or insincere. Most dated me for my fame or the headlines of being with me. I'd also tried dating outside of the entertainment industry, but that had been a disaster. One date had spent the entire time taking selfies and posting to social media about being with me. Another time, paparazzi followed me and my date, and the woman finally ditched me, crying. That was when I'd started to wear a hat when I went out, but I'd given up on dating for a while, until now.

Leading her into the building, we took the elevator to the third floor, and I guided Evy towards the room with my hand on the small of her back. It was the most spacious room at the resort, overlooking the pool and including a view of the sea. The room also had both a balcony and a private bathing terrace. It was quite cool in the room from being shut up all day. Beyond the sitting area, a king-size bed dominated the space.

Entering the room, I led Evy over to the sitting area, which surprised her. She gave me a quizzical glance when I gestured for her to sit. Holding her hands, I sat on the beige sofa next to her and stated, "Before we go any further, I need to talk to you. I've enjoyed every single minute of our time together over the last three days. You're everything I've ever dreamed of in a woman and never thought I'd find."

"I can't look at you without feeling it. Whatever this is. It's not just attraction. It's you... all of you. And I don't know if it's love, because I've never known what that feels like. But I know it's something I don't want to lose." I cupped her cheek in my hand.

Evy admitted, "I feel the same about you. I've been married before, but it clearly didn't work out. I thought I loved him, but that proved to be untrue."

I took a deep breath. My hand caressed her cheek softly. A flicker of worry was clear in Evy's eyes.

Clasping both her hands again, I stared down at them and carried on. "I haven't been completely honest about myself. Everything I've told you has been the truth, except I've left out a few details. My name is George Henry Starling. As I've mentioned, I've been called Henry since I was a young child. I'm an actor, but I made it sound like I'm just a two-bit actor. But I'm not. I'm a famous actor. The world knows me as Ace Starling, star of the Vigil Warden movies."

I stopped and glanced at Evy. She stared at me in confusion, disbelief, and shock. Her blue eyes were wide, and she seemed to hold her breath.

I swiftly added, "I wanted you to see the real me, not the one the tabloids and papers have created." Letting go of one hand, I took out my phone and pulled up a picture from my last movie premiere. "I wear contacts when filming, and I've cut my hair. Otherwise, we wouldn't have been able to tour the island unhindered."

When I showed her the photo of myself as Ace Starling, Evy gasped, seeing that I was telling the truth. She let go of my hand and sat back, putting space between the two of us. "I need a moment to think."

"I understand. You can take as long as you need," I told her.

Evy walked over to the balcony door and out onto the balcony to the railing, shutting the door behind her. I let her go, knowing that following her at this time could wreck the fragility of our relationship. I ran a hand through my hair, slumping back onto the sofa. Sighing, I'd done my best to explain and hoped she would accept my sincerity.

It was almost ten minutes later when Evy came back inside and sat down on the sofa next to me. Not as close as she had been before, but the fact alone that she had not left made me happy. "I need you to explain from when we first met and tell me everything. Also, if you lied or changed anything, tell me the truth."

I let out a sigh of relief. "I was snorkeling near my yacht when we first met. Originally, I had planned to stay on my yacht during my time here, but once I met you, I watched you return to shore and saw where you were staying. I made the choice to stay here to get to know you better. You're the reason I'm at this resort."

Evy gave me a look of disbelief. "You got a room here just because of me?"

"That's right, sweetheart. When I realized you didn't know who I was, I wanted to get to know you better as just me. It was freeing. I didn't expect it to become more, but hoped it would," I stated.

Wide-eyed, she challenged me. "You realize how crazy that sounds, right?"

I threw my hands up in the air. "I know! I've never done anything so spontaneous or nuts in my entire life. But if I hadn't, I wouldn't have gotten to know you." I placed my hands on either side of her face, risking touching her when I didn't know if she was mad at me or not.

Evy sat back again, pulling out of my hands. "I'm still not sure. Let me take a walk. I feel like I need to clear my head."

She stood up and walked to the door of the suite. I sat in a bit of shock. As she opened the door, I didn't notice her glance back to see that I was exactly as when she had stood up.

I heard the door close, and it snapped me out of my frozen state. *Had I just lost the love of my life? Wait?Did I truly love her? If I did, I couldn't let Evy just walk away!*

Jumping up, I ran out the door, looking to see where she was. Not catching a glance of her, I ran down the stairs and down to the first floor, peering around the pool area before heading for the gate. Outside the gate, I saw her walking around the edge of the building, heading towards the front of the resort.

"Evy!" I called as I ran faster towards her.

She whipped around, hearing her name. Her mouth dropped open in surprise.

I caught up with her in just a moment. "Please don't leave." I pulled her to me, wrapping my arms around her waist.

"I told you I was just going for a walk. I was coming back," Evy mumbled the words from where her face was pressed against my chest. She lifted her hands so that she could push herself back.

With a shaking hand, I brushed a piece of hair back and behind Evy's ear. "When I saw you had left, I thought you were gone for good. That's when I realized I couldn't let you go. If I did, my heart would break. I couldn't let you go."

Suddenly, Evy leaned forward, closing the distance between us, and kissed me. Her arms twined around my neck. This was one of the first times she'd started anything between us, let alone such a passionate kiss. It took me completely by surprise.

Leaning back slightly with her arms still around my neck and her body pressed to mine, Evy whispered against my lips, "That was the most amazing thing you could've said. Let's go back to your room."

In the room, I reached down to take Evy's shoes off. I slowly caressed her feet, massaging the soles. I then stood up and spun her around to ease the zipper of her dress down. The sound of the zipper almost echoed in the room, which was quiet except for the sound of our breathing. Reaching for the edges, I slid the dress off her shoulders until it tumbled down to her feet, leaving her in only a lacy burgundy bra and matching panties that were similar in color to the shoes she had worn.

Rotating her, I fell to my knees and leaned forward to rest my forehead on Evy's stomach. I inhaled the perfume that had been driving me crazy all day and nuzzled her soft skin. She reached out and wrapped her arms lightly around my head.

"I'm sorry that my body isn't perfect. It has stretch marks from carrying twins."

I lifted my head to kiss the stretch marks she was referring to. I hadn't even seen them until she'd mentioned them. The thin, silvery lines across her stomach were just proof of how incredible a woman she was to have carried and birthed two human beings. Initially, I'd been too busy celebrating the beauty of her body and the fact that she'd accepted my revelation to notice them.

"You are perfect in every way, simply because you are you. These are just a part of you, symbols of your motherhood."

I leaned back to peel off my suit jacket and then belt. Evy reached out to tug off my t-shirt. "No wonder you never suggested swimming," she murmured, trailing her fingers through the dark hair on my chest. She then admired the ridges of defined muscles, her palms sliding down to the waistband.

I groaned and lifted Evy, walking over to the bed. I laid her down, shed the rest of my clothes in a blur, and stood beside the bed completely bare. Evy looked up at me, eyes wide yet hungry before her gaze traveled the length of me, taking in how ready I was for her. I watched as her mouth partly opened and her breath became shallow.

I eased her panties down, then reached behind her, fingers deft against the clasp of her bra. Both hit the floor, forgotten for now. I crawled up onto the bed, kneeling over her, then sat back, looking at Evy's naked body in adoration and almost a look of ravenousness.

Evy reached out, put a hand behind my head and brought me down for a deep kiss, her tongue playing with mine. I had to rest my body weight on my hands to prevent pressing down on her. Both of us moaned in need as the kiss deepened. I sank onto one elbow as I took her breast in one hand — a perfect fit — and molded it. My other hand took a handful of hair while I moved to kiss and nibble at her ear. Evy grabbed at my back and arched hers. I smirked and chuckled, realizing I'd found one of her erogenous zones. When her hands moved to my backside, pulling my groin to hers in desperation, I sat up and held her hands still.

I struggled to talk between gasps. "I had hoped for our first time to be slow... This is moving too quickly."

"What if this is what I want, what I need?" Evy demanded while she panted. She hauled me back down to her, reaching between us to hold me in her palm.

A sudden thought made me stop. "How long has it been, Evy?"

She pulled her lip between her teeth for a moment before answering. "Before I had my twins."

Her honesty tugged at my heart. I also realized that this first time could be fast since it had been a while for her...and me. I hadn't been in a relationship for a few years. And I wasn't a person for one-night stands.

Evy still held me in her hand. She moved her hands to my shoulders and pulled me forward. Her need was obvious.

Before I got too lost, I had to be sensible. "Protection?" I asked her.

"Pill," she blurted out quickly as she continued to pull me closer.

I groaned as I slid into her, the heat of her body stealing my breath. We sighed in unison as we fit together perfectly. I moved as Evy rocked opposite me. Her body clenched against mine, drawing me deeper. She panted harder, and I groaned as our rhythm quickened, her body tightening around me as we pushed each other higher.

As I had expected, soon I could feel Evy's body quickening around mine. I wasn't far behind either. Evy screamed as she climaxed, and I stiffened and jerked with my own.

As our heartbeats slowed down, I rolled to the side and gathered Evy's body to me. To admit that I'd never experienced such next level raw, overwhelming sex was an understatement. I pressed a kiss to Evy's hair and brushed it away from her face. She shifted slightly to smile at me.

"That was ..." I couldn't find the words.

Evy's only reply was "Mmm."

I reached down and wrested the covers up over both of us. There would be more time to talk, and to make love again slowly, in the morning, or during the night.

Evy

I awoke to see Henry's naked backside standing next to the bed as he hung up the phone. I admired it as I stretched, feeling a slight soreness between my legs. Finished with the call, Henry pivoted around and climbed back into bed, gathering me to him upon seeing that I was awake. He kissed my nose, brushed my cheek with a fingertip, then said, "I ordered breakfast, sweetheart. I hope I wasn't being presumptuous."

I shook my head no to his question and reflected on the night before when I'd taken time to think outside on the balcony. Initially, I'd wrestled with my emotions, trying to digest what Henry had revealed. I'd thought about how he had lied to me. *But had he?* He had told me the truth, but not all of it, leaving out pieces.

Henry had said he was an actor, but he was obviously more than just a basic one. People knew him as Ace Starling, the mega-star of the screen. His eyes were green, unlike in the movies and seen at premieres. He had cut his hair short to change his look, too. I had initially wondered whether all this mattered. It didn't change who he was. I'd ended up wrestling with one question—Did it change how I felt about him?

I had stayed outside for ten minutes, thinking about that question. Leaning on the balcony railing, I'd stared out at the view of the sea. My emotions were all over the place. I was upset with him for not having confided the truth to me from the beginning. On the other hand, I had never had such feelings, even for my ex-husband.

Ultimately, I had decided that the answer was no. But I needed to know the entire story from Henry. So I'd headed inside to talk to him. Even after hearing him explain more of his side, I had not been ready to forgive him quite yet. I had meant to use the walk as a chance to calm down and finish working through my thoughts. When Henry had run after me and confessed his fears of my leaving, it had broken through my last resistance.

As I leaned back into him, remembering last night, pressing against him, hearing a groan, which made me grin at him over my shoulder.

I remembered how I'd woken in the middle of the night and checked if his nipples were as sensitive as mine. I'd discovered they were, and this had woken him. We'd made love again, this time with me on top. Making love with him was phenomenal; everything I'd thought it should be and never was with my ex-husband.

Henry pinched my bottom, saying, "Stop that, you minx. I need to ask you a serious question."

I rolled over to look at him questioningly.

He rested his head on his hand, elbow on the pillow, and said, "Would you like to stay with me in my room? I can have my personal assistant cancel your room and move your things for you."

"You have a personal assistant?" This piece of information distracted me.

"His name's Erik Matig," Henry confirmed, and then he playfully touched my nose. "Pay atten-tion to the question."

I thought for a moment. "Since we've been to-gether for the past two days and are now sleep-ing together, one room makes more sense. Are you sure you want to do this with someone you've known for not even three days?"

Henry looked at me. "Evy, I'm in love with you. Three days, three weeks, three months, or three years. I've never felt this way about anyone. Ever."

"I love you as well. I can't believe I'm saying this. We shouldn't feel this way after three days."

Reaching out, Henry placed his hands on either side of my face and gently kissed me. As he did so, my stomach growled. Before he could say or do anything else, there was a knock on the door. I twisted my head to look towards the door as Henry said, "Perfect timing. That's our food."

We both got out of bed and put on the robes provided by the resort. Henry answered the door while I went into the bathroom to straighten my hair as best as I could with the comb I found there. It had become quite a mess from our nighttime activities. When we both sat down to eat, we discovered we were starving upon smelling the food.

Within the hour, there was another knock at the door. Henry answered the door and introduced me to Erik. He was a slim, mid-height, early-thirties man with a brown crew cut and brown eyes. When Erik came in, I tightened my robe and looked away from him, wondering what the assistant thought of me, a woman that his boss had just met, now sharing his room. Instead, Erik surprised me by treating me with respect and kindness, with no hint of judgment or disgust.

He brought in my luggage and said that a maid had packed my things while he watched to prevent theft. He thanked me for sharing the lock code and handed me the personal items I had put in the safe. Erik also assured me he'd canceled the room and that the resort would credit the remaining nights back to me. My mouth dropped open in astonishment, since I hadn't thought that was possible.

I thanked Erik for his help, and he smiled politely and then said goodbye. Henry told me to put my things wherever I wanted in the closet and bureau. He'd be in the shower, waiting for me. It didn't take me long to hang up and fold my clothes next to his, then set out my toiletries in the bathroom. Everything felt so natural: waking up next to Henry, breakfast, even putting my things beside his. I set out my clothes for after the shower, took the toiletries I needed there, and then I went to join him.

Henry gathered me into his arms and let the water cascade over us both. He helped wash my hair and body since he had already washed up. His hands lingered over every part of me until we were both breathless and gasping. He twisted off the water, handed me a towel, and dried himself off. Once dry, he drew me back into his arms and leaned down to bite me gently on the neck. He tugged me toward the bed, whispering, "You make me hungry for you."

Later, after dinner, once again courtesy of room service, we lay out on the terrace looking at the stars. Sharing a single lounger, I lay half sideways between his legs with my head pillowed on Henry's chest. Henry rested his chin on my head and twisted his fingers in my hair. The sounds of Magaluf drifted around us, but we were solidly in our own world. We discussed our lives back in the States, both of us avoiding the topic of my departure in four days.

Chapter 5

Evy

For the next three days, we spent all our time together. We wasted one day away on Henry's yacht, driving around the waters of Mallorca. I even tried deep-sea fishing.

"Hold on to the pole, pull back, and crank the reel!" Henry called to me as he rushed across the deck.

Turning to look at him, I yelled back, "What do you think I'm doing!"

Struggling with the giant fishing pole, I staggered forward and back against the resistance of the fish pulling on it. I'd fished in the lakes back home, but this was nothing like that at all! My feet slipped just as Henry reached me.

"Whoa!" I cried out as I fell to the deck.

Henry tried to grab me, but he slipped as well. We both tumbled down in a mess of limbs, laughing. Later, he slathered me with aloe to help with the slight sunburn I got from not putting on enough sunscreen.

That day, Henry shared with me the reason he'd originally come to Mallorca. It'd been to have time to think. He needed to make a life-changing decision about his career and thought this was where he could relax and make it.

"The reason for my trip to Mallorca was to help me decide whether I'll keep making Vigil Warden movies and how long I should stay in the franchise. They gave me an offer to make one more major film, but also to do a series with that role. However, I don't want to be the actor who's riding on the coattails of that singular role."

He paused to glance out over the sea, where the yacht was drifting. "Look at Harrison Ford. He did great with Indiana Jones, yet he went on to craft other iconic characters. Do I want to take that one last movie deal, then wait to see what I'm offered? See if I can pick the movies that I'd like to do? Would I rather still make movie after movie or do the series and continually be working? Having met you, sweetheart," he paused and kissed me, "I'm leaning toward the possibility of a final Vigil Warden movie before retiring from the role and selecting films I want to act in. It may mean that I may have lulls between films, but I'm financially secure–that's not an issue. Mostly, I want to have the time to spend with you as well as Matthew and Cora."

His including my children thrilled me. I was excited to go back home to tell my mom and aunt about Henry. After my divorce, they had encouraged me to date again, but I hadn't been interested. I wasn't sure how to tell Matthew and Cora about Henry because of them being only three years old. How would they understand Mommy had a boyfriend?

HENRY

I reserved a private beach for us, and we spent the whole day there. This time, I made sure to put sunscreen on Evy before we spent time in the sun.

"Aren't you done yet? I swear you're putting more on me than I've ever had on before." Evy complained to me.

Looking at her over my sunglasses, I wanted to make sure I covered every inch of her. I didn't want to see her baked in the Mediterranean sun. We had an umbrella up, but I doubted she was going to stay under it the entire day.

"Do you always complain this much?" I asked her as I leaned over to kiss her. She swatted at me as if I were an annoying fly.

"Only when someone tries to turn me into a greased pig," Evy said back.

Grabbing her, my hands slipped, and I fell against her, knocking her down onto the towel. As we landed, we began laughing. It quickly turned into gasps and heavy breathing as my hands slid across her body.

The bikini that Evy wore bared more than it hid. I'd admired it when she had removed the cover she had brought with her. The swimsuit was a bandeau strapless top and low-waist bottom in a teal color with a tropical print. The moment she let the cover fall away, something in me shifted. My focus locked on her, taking in more than I should have, and I had to force myself to breathe normally. I wanted to reach for her, to close the distance, but I held back, gripping control tighter than I expected to need.

"Henry," Evy gasped, then giggled. "Stop. Please."

Running my lips down her neck, I asked. "Why? We're both enjoying this."

"Because there is sand getting into my hair and bikini," she told me with a smirk on her face.

I leaned up on my hands and looked around to see she was right. The towel had become skewed, and there was sand all over it. If we continued, it would go to places neither of us wanted.

With a loud chuckle, I lifted myself off Evy, then pulled her up too. I lifted the towel to shake the sand off. As I did so, the wind shifted, and heard a shriek.

"Ahh!" Evy cried out as the breeze blew the sand right at her.

Dropping the towel, I hurried to apologize. "I'm so sorry, Evy! I didn't mean to get sand all over you!"

I rushed over to where she stood hunched over to find her giggling into her arm. Evy then threw herself onto me and rubbed the sand from her body onto mine.

"Ugh, how dare you!" I teased.

Evy ran away from me down the beach. I followed in pursuit, catching up as she tripped and fell into the waves with a shout. I reached out to her as she came up, coughing but smiling.

Evy stammered around the coughs, "Well, that was graceless."

Hugging her, I proceeded to help her rinse off the sand. That led to her helping me, and we ended up making love in the water.

EVY

On our last full day together, we depleted ourselves making love, rejuvenated with food, and lay in the room ignoring the world outside. That evening, Henry and I enjoyed dinner delivered from a nearby local restaurant. We had a cheese board, sea bass ceviche, and gnocchi with pesto sauce to share.

After dinner that evening, Henry tried to get me to stay.

Holding me close, he pleaded with me. "I'll book the room for another week. Don't worry about your return plane ticket; I'll give you the money. You can use my private jet to go home."

He was desperate for any way to spend more time together.

Twisting in his arms, I gave him a sad smile. I just couldn't. As much as I loved Henry and our time together, I desperately missed my kids.

I'd tried to do video streaming with them the first couple of days I'd been in Mallorca, but it had been too difficult and made the twins cry. I remembered the last time I tried and the conversation with my mother.

"Mom, please, just turn the camera off and let's try talking on speaker instead." I couldn't bear looking at the faces of my children, who were sobbing.

I watched as my phone screen went black and heard my mom coax my daughter. "Cora, talk to Mommy."

Instead, the crying from my daughter had just gotten louder. It made me feel like a horrible mother for taking the trip to be by myself, even though I knew my kids were being well taken care of. I also knew that soon after the phone call was over, both twins would be back to their happy selves.

"Mom, it's okay. Don't force her. I love you, Cora. I love you, Matthew. Mommy will be home before you know it. Take me off speaker now, please," I told my mom. Once I knew the kids couldn't hear, I spoke just to my mother. "I can't do this anymore. From here on, I'll record a video every day and text it to you to show them. If they want to record one back, do that and send it to me."

My mother had agreed to this plan, and it had worked better. I had sent videos every day, and every other day the twins had sent one to me.

Now I needed to return to reality, even if that meant being without Henry, for however long it took for us to figure things out. Henry and I had discussed how we could maintain our relationship after leaving Mallorca. We agreed it wouldn't be easy, but neither of us wanted to let go of what we'd discovered together.

Because Henry was between movies, his acting schedule was currently up in the air. Plus, neither of us wanted the demands of a star to affect me or the twins. The time involved in my job and as a mom also needed to be considered, as well as the twins' routine. Neither of us wanted to upset that.

What followed was a sleepless night. It alternated between a frantic need driving us to savor every moment together and a desperate desire to fill the remaining hours together. My flight would leave mid-morning the next day.

HENRY

The alarm went off, but the two of us lay in each other's arms a while longer, unwilling to let reality into our paradise. My fingers drifted up and down Evy's arm. The two of us were quiet, neither willing to speak and break the silence. Evy had mostly packed her bag, except for the items she needed that morning. It wouldn't take long for her to get ready. I had pre-ordered room service to deliver breakfast, and it was waiting in the room service cubby.

Finally, we both knew we had to get up. Evy took a shower while I set up breakfast. Once dressed, Evy packed up her remaining items and set her suitcase by the door. She strolled back to the table and sat down to eat. Each bite seemed to be a countdown to her leaving. I held her hand while we ate, the only sound being the silverware against the plates and the sips from cups.

Evy finished her coffee while I took a quick shower and dressed. I was taking her to the airport in a taxi, which we met at the resort lobby. We kept our silence from the hotel all the way to the airport. Evy sat with her head on my shoulder while I had my arm around her. We clasped our other hands together. I rubbed my thumb across the back of her hand in a gesture meant to soothe us both. The separation to come was being felt heavily by the two of us. We didn't know when we would see each other again.

When it was time to leave the taxi, we kissed, and our clasped hands let go slowly as she pried herself away. Evy kept her gaze on me, our eyes locked until she went through the door to the security area. Once out of sight, Evy would give in to the tears that had been threatening. They would last well after the plane had taken off, and she watched the airport disappear from view with them spilling down her face. I stood at the gate until after the plane had taxied and then flown away before heading back to the resort. Being alone in "our" room held too many memories, so I checked out and went back to my yacht.

After two days of wandering around the yacht, Erik cornered me.

"Why are we still here in Mallorca?" he asked. "Evy left two days ago, and you're moping around."

It snapped me out of my funk. "Have my jet ready to leave tonight. Schedule for the yacht to be moored and stored later in the day. Before that, we need to go to Soller. I have an errand that I need to do there."

I didn't know how I'd do it, but I had to figure out how I could have Evy in my life. Not just once in a while, but every day. It would take some figuring out, but I was determined. First, though, there was a stop at one last place in Soller I had to go before I left.

Chapter 6

EVY

Just three days after being home, I found myself checking for texts and phone calls constantly. I was supposed to be working on my planning while the preschoolers were napping. Instead, here I was, staring at my phone. With a sigh, I flipped it over so I couldn't see the screen. I could count the number of times I'd snuck a peek at it on both hands.

"Damn," I swore under my breath, then looked around at the children lying near me to see if they had heard.

With a sigh, I swiveled my desk chair to face the window. I hadn't called or texted Henry, even though I had his number. I didn't want to be the first to make contact. The physical distance between us had dimmed the certainty I had about his feelings for me. He had my number, and I didn't know what he had planned to do after I left. I hadn't thought to ask. Now I worried maybe it wasn't all I'd thought, even though we had talked about trying to make things work.

Why did it bother me so much that he hadn't contacted me when I hadn't asked him to and he hadn't promised?

Another sigh escaped before I could stop it. I had to stop moping and focus on the present. Right now, I had to write up my plans for next week's class lessons. I turned back to my desk, but couldn't resist one more glance at my phone.

After being home for a week, I felt as though Mallorca was just a dream. I'd become swept up in the everyday life of being a mom, teacher, daughter, and niece. It was as if nothing had changed while I'd been gone. But for me, my whole inner being had changed. Initially, I had kept details to myself, but later told my mom, Maeve, and aunt Eileen about meeting the man of my dreams in Mallorca. I told them his name was Henry but didn't tell them who he really was. I didn't want them to contact him, because they would. They'd already tried to get so many details from me about him.

I came home with my twins from the daycare center where I worked to find the main door open to my house, but the screen door closed and a strange black sedan parked out front. I didn't recognize it, but the brand was one I knew was pricey. *Whose could it be?*

I walked into my house and through the living room that led straight to the kitchen, where I found both my mother and aunt sitting at the kitchen table with Henry! I stopped so quickly in shock that the twins ran into me.

"Henry!"

"Yes, Henry's here!" my mother declared with a smile on her face and a twinkle in her eye. She obviously enjoyed the shock on my face.

"Why didn't you say he was so handsome?" Aunt Eileen wondered.

"Indeed, what's the reason?" Henry responded, his own eyes sparkling. He was wearing a pair of jeans with a gray henley top, along with a hat. Though casually dressed, he still exuded some of the same appeal that had drawn me to him when I first met him. In contrast, I felt disheveled in jeans and a t-shirt that had paint at the edge of the cuffs from doing art with the preschoolers and a messy bun that probably looked like a bird's nest after the workday.

I pushed a piece of hair behind my ear from where it had fallen out of the bun and across my face, walked into the kitchen, and inquired, "When did you arrive?"

Holding up a glass of water that he had, Henry replied, "Approximately twenty minutes ago. Your mom and aunt were kind enough to let me in when they saw me sitting in my car. They also gave me some water."

"Certainly they were," I muttered under my breath. "It would be better to interrogate you then."

Henry stood up and walked over, pecking me on the cheek. He spoke into my ear so only I could hear, "You look great, sweetheart. I missed you. Did you miss me?"

I blushed and didn't know what to say back. Before I could say anything, Henry kneeled next to me and said, "These must be Matthew and Cora. I am so excited about finally meeting you. I've got gifts for the two of you."

"Presents?" asked Cora excitedly.

"Me want!" Matthew demanded.

"It's 'I want,' not 'me want,'" I corrected automatically, rolling my eyes, then told my son, "Matthew, you don't demand gifts. You need to ask nicely."

"Pleeeease," Matthew pleaded.

Henry laughed and stood up. "How do I refuse that? Do you want to help me get them out of the car?"

Both twins nodded and ran out of the house ahead of him.

"You didn't have to get them something," I said.

"I'm aware, but I wanted to," Henry clarified as he followed the twins out the door and to his car. He came back carrying two bags. He set one down in front of each twin. "They can go ahead and open them."

"Mommy?" questioned Matthew as he looked at me.

I nodded. "It's okay to open them."

The twins tore into the bags like whirling dervishes. There was an explosion of tissue paper everywhere! Matthew loved the robot he received, and Cora loved the baby doll. I looked at Henry with love in my eyes. The thought he had put into getting my children's gifts was clear. The twins immediately played with their new toys. I made a sound in my throat, and the twins stopped to look up at me, then Henry.

"Thank you!" they both chimed in unison.

Henry laughed again. "My pleasure. I'm glad you like the gifts."

He drew me to his side, giving me a hug.

My mom and Aunt Eileen looked on, glancing between the two of us and then at each other. It was obvious there was more going on between Henry and me than I had described.

Henry looked over at Maeve and Eileen. "Thanks for staying here with me while I waited for Evy. Since the twins are busy, would you mind watching them while we take a walk?"

I led Henry out the door and around the back of the house to a wooded area that bordered my property. We walked next to each other for a while before Henry spoke. "I hope you don't mind my coming without telling you. Especially since we haven't talked since the airport. I've been fairly busy."

"It's fine. I assumed you were busy with your contracts or figuring out what you were go-ing to do with the movie. Or another part of your life in New York." I didn't look at him as I spoke, instead watching my feet as I kicked at the dirt and other bits covering the path. The forest blurred at the edges as my thoughts cir-cled, pulling apart old assumptions and holding them up against what he'd just said, searching for something that made sense.

"I had to handle some things, such as the movie things we spoke about. I also wanted to think about and figure out how we'd make this relationship work. Evy, I want this to work," Henry said, stopping and spinning me to look up at him and see his face. "After leaving Mallorca, I spent four days in New York before I could sort everything out, and then it took me two days to drive here."

I bit my lip nervously before confessing, "When I didn't hear from you I thought maybe you'd decided this was just a fling after all."

"Evy, you are far more important to me than just a fling. You're my life!" He hauled me into his arms, hugging me tightly and then drawing back to kiss me. His lips were so familiar to me that I felt as if I'd been kissing them all my life.

"I want us to be a family–me, you, Matthew, and Cora," he went on. "The new Vigil Warden movie will start filming next year, giving me about six months before we begin pre-production. I want to spend that time with you and the twins. I have some things that I'll need to do in both New York and Hollywood, but primarily I plan to be here."

My heartbeat sped up, and my head started to spin. *Henry living here with us? How was I going to explain that? Isn't that what I wanted though?*

"Is that alright? Am I moving too fast?" Henry questioned.

I admitted honestly, "I don't know. I mean, I want you here. I do. But here, in my house? That's what I'm unsure about. How do I explain that to the twins? And I'll have to tell their father. There are so many pieces and parts involved."

"That thought never occurred to me," Henry said, "I'm sorry. How it would affect your life wasn't part of my planning. I could rent a place in town instead?" I could tell Henry didn't have his heart in the offer, but he made it anyway. We kept walking, this time, Henry taking my hand to hold it in his.

I thought and then said, "I need to think about this, Henry." Finally, I asked him, "How long do you intend to stay here?"

"I hadn't decided. My schedule is clear for the next three weeks." We had continued walking but turned around to head back towards the house since we'd gone to the back of the lot. I glanced at the lot behind my house. It was extremely large, but undeveloped. Where it ended, there was another large lot that was completely wooded. I'd always wondered about it but never gotten around to figuring out who owned it or finding out why they had never built on it.

"Perhaps staying in town for a week would be good. That'd give me time to talk to Vincent, the twins' dad. I'd also like him to meet you. You could spend more time with the twins, too. If all goes well, then we could see about your moving in after that. How does that sound?"

"That sounds like a really good plan. A week would give us time to see how everything feels—for you, for me, and for the twins. We can take it one step at a time and decide what makes sense after that. And if it works for you, maybe we could find a little time to ourselves while I'm there, but only if you're comfortable. I've really been missing you." This last piece

Henry murmured against my ear as he turned to me and kissed me deeply. He ran his hands down my sides and then back up again.

I leaned into Henry and kissed him back. It was amazing how quickly the spark ignited between us again. By the time we broke apart, we were both panting. All over a simple kiss.

I leaned my head against his chest. "I'll ask."

HENRY

After returning to the house, I said goodbye and then called Erik to have him help me find a place to stay in town for the next week. I asked him to send me more luggage as I'd only packed an overnight bag. I also said to overnight it wherever he found for me to stay. I'd driven my car to Michigan from New York, which had been a very long drive, but I'd wanted to have my own vehicle here since I was planning to stay for quite some time. The drive itself would've taken just under twelve hours, but I'd broken it up into two days so I wouldn't arrive in the evening and tire myself out with too many hours behind the wheel of the car.

It took less than an hour for Erik to call me back with the information about the rental and when my luggage would arrive. I first went to check out the place he found for my stay and texted the info to Evy. She texted a reply, asking if I wanted to come to her house for dinner. I accepted and asked if I could bring anything. Evy told me no and also said, "everyone" would be there. I wondered exactly what that meant.

Arriving at Evy's house for the second time that day, I had to park my car this time next to three other cars. I recognized Evy's gray sedan from earlier. There was also a flashy red two-door sporty car and a bronze minivan.

I knocked at the door after moving the bouquet I'd bought from one hand to the other. When I went to buy it, I realized I didn't know what Evy's favorite flower was, so I'd bought traditional red roses.

I never expected a man to open the door. This one was the same height as me, with blonde hair and blue eyes. With a laugh, he greeted me, "Welcome, come on in, you must be Henry!" I put out my hand; the man grasped it, shook it, and then tugged me into the house.

Evy was just coming into the living area from the kitchen. She was also laughing and chasing a little girl who had a face full of frosting. "Come back; I need to clean your face!"

The man wheeled to see who Evy was after. "Henry is here now. I'll take care of Geneva."

Evy looked at me with a big smile. "Hey."

I shifted from foot to foot. I wasn't sure why, but I was uncomfortable. Where things had been natural before, I now felt unsure with the other man here.

"Here, these are for you." It seemed like I was announcing the fact to her rather than stating it as I handed her the roses.

"Thank you," Evy responded before heading to the kitchen, checking if I was behind her. "I'm going to put them in some water."

Following her into the kitchen, I spotted a second man sitting in the living area on the couch with the twins on either side of him while he read a book. He had brown hair and looked similar to the children. *Is that Vincent, the twins' father?* If that was Vincent though, who was the other guy?

In the kitchen, I saw Evy's mom and aunt setting the dining table for six people, and there was a smaller table to the side with three kids' settings. A bowl of salad, spaghetti, bread, and a cake filled the kitchen counter.

"Henry, could you grab the vase from that high cabinet?" Evy asked, pointing.

"Yes," I said, opening the cabinet and giving her the vase.

Maeve told me, "The flowers are beautiful."

"The table looks lovely with them," agreed Eileen, as Evy set the vase in the middle of the dining room table.

I sheepishly explained, "I wasn't sure what flowers you liked, so I just picked up roses."

"I love them," Evy said, smiling at me. "Roses are beautiful. My favorite flowers are lilacs, which are hard to buy and bring as a bouquet. I'd love any flowers you bring me anytime, Henry."

Evy took my hand, continuing, "Let me introduce you around. You know my mom and aunt already."

We walked back into the living area and over to the man on the couch with the twins. "This is Vincent. Vincent, this is Henry. Henry, I've told you about Vincent. He's my ex-husband and the twins' dad."

I reached out my hand to Vincent. "It is nice to meet you, Vincent."

Vincent shook my hand and replied, "Likewise." It was obvious he was sizing me up. But that was fine because I was doing the same to him. He struck me as someone who considered himself a man's man. From what Evy had told me, I already had a sense of how that had felt on the other side of it.

His handshake was firm, too firm, his grip tightening like he had something to prove. I met it without backing down.

"Daddy, Henry gave me dolly and Matthew ro-bot!" exclaimed Cora.

"It was just a small hello gift," I said.

"I see," said Vincent.

Evy must've sensed that things were getting tense between the two of us because she pulled my arm and said, "Come over here and meet my best friend."

We headed to a room that was obviously the twins' bedroom. There was the man who had let me in and the little girl who had had frosting on her face.

"Henry, this is my best friend, Jonathan, and his daughter, Geneva."

Jonathan reached out his hand again, this time for a fist bump. "Nice to officially meet you."

Evy led me back out of the bedroom, and I hung around in the kitchen until dinner was ready. I wasn't comfortable in the living room with her ex there.

The rest of dinner went well, even though Vin-cent maintained his glare at me for a good portion of the time. After Evy glared at him, though, Vincent seemed to take the hint and relaxed a little, staring at the table instead. I was glad because I had been about to kick the man under the table. I could tell that his attitude had been upsetting Evy, and that made me unhappy.

Jonathan was a genuinely great person, and I hit it off with him immediately. He and I were both football fans, though unfortunately we rooted for different teams. I found out he was also a sci-fi fiction reader, and we ended up having a discussion about authors. Of course, our biggest connection was Evy. These made us practically best friends by the end of the evening. Evy seemed to consider the evening a success and was happy with how things went between everyone. She also seemed pleasantly surprised by the flowers that I had brought.

EVY

Even though dinner had gone well, something still wouldn't settle. My mind kept drifting ahead to Monday, to work, to the classroom, to the twins' routine waiting for me to step back into it like nothing had changed. Except something had. Henry didn't fit anywhere in that picture. I stared down at my hands, turning one over in the other as I tried to make sense of it. He had said he had three weeks. Three weeks before what? Before he left? Before whatever life he had outside of this pulled him away again? My chest tightened at the thought, and I pressed my lips together, forcing myself to stop before my thoughts spiraled any further. There were too many questions, and not nearly enough answers.

Sunday felt easier.

Henry slipped into everything without hesitation, into the morning routines, the noise, the constant motion of the house. He crouched beside Matthew to help with his shoes, laughed when Cora spilled juice down her shirt, and carried things into the kitchen when my mom asked, as if it was second nature. At the restaurant, he slid into the booth beside me, his hand finding mine under the table without even look-ing. There were no awkward pauses, no uncer-tainty. He was simply there.

I caught myself watching him more than once, trying to understand how someone who felt so natural in my life could still feel so uncertain in my future. In these small, ordinary moments, it felt like he belonged here. And that was what unsettled me the most.

That evening, after I'd put the children to bed, Henry and I were relaxing on the couch in the living room. I'd snuggled next to him with my legs curled up on the cushions. Henry draped his arm over my shoulder, crossing his ankles and resting them on the coffee table in front of the couch. I'd decided I had to talk to him about the questions that I'd thought about the day before. Turning my head to glance up at him, I caught his attention.

"Tomorrow I work until 4 pm. The twins go to preschool with me most days. What are your plans for the day and week?" I asked hesitantly.

"Well, tomorrow I thought I'd get to know the town. Besides the places you've taken me, I don't really know what is around the area."

I twisted on the couch to face Henry. "If you'd like, I can make a list of places you might be interested in. It would make it easier than just bringing up the map or trying to search on your phone. I can also give you suggestions for other areas and places to visit in nearby towns. It may take you a couple of days though, with the number I've in my head already."

Smiling, Henry reached out to hug me. "That sounds great! I'd love it if you made a list for me. I'll plan to explore Monday and Tuesday then. Besides making it easier, anything from you is special." I blushed at his words. "As for the rest of the week, I need to check in with Erik at some point, so maybe I'll do that on Thursday. I'd also like to spend time with Matthew and Cora. Would that be possible?"

"Hmm, let me think," I paused. "Are you sure you want to handle both on your own? Have you ever watched or taken two children out by yourself?" I raised an eyebrow as I asked this.

"You think *the* Vigil Warden can't keep a rein on two youngsters after saving the world five times?" Leaning forward, Henry tickled me as he used his actor's voice to answer my question.

In between my laughter, I blurted, "Stop, I'm being serious! Honey, you've no idea how much energy, time, and chaos are involved when taking on my two hooligans."

"Did you just call me 'honey'?"

I blushed. As when Henry had first called me sweetheart, 'honey' had just come out. I hadn't even realized it until he asked me about it.

Henry brushed his knuckles across my reddened cheek. "I like it." He grinned at me, then resumed, "Honestly, no, I've never watched kids before. But I won't know how I'll do until I've had the chance, will I?"

"True. Fine. Maybe on Wednesday you can take the twins. We'll figure out in a couple of days what you can do with them unless you come up with your own plan," I said as I straightened my top, which had become twisted from the tickling.

I settled back against Henry. The talk had gone better than I'd expected. Things were going too easily, and something had to go wrong eventually.

Chapter 7

HENRY

Monday, Evy went back to work, and I had the day to myself. I ended up walking through Belding with no known destination, just following the sidewalks wherever they led. A couple of people nodded as I passed, one older man lifting two fingers from the brim of his cap in greeting. Someone held the door open for me at a small café without a word, just a quick smile before they stepped aside. No one asked who I was, but I caught the second look, the quiet curiosity. It reminded me of home.

Not the place itself, but the way people were. Open without being intrusive. Friendly, without expectation. I hadn't realized how much I missed that until I was standing in the middle of it again.

The next day, I drove farther out, following the list Evy had written for me. One stop turned into three, then five. I found a trail that cut through a stretch of trees just beginning to turn, the air cool and still enough that every step sounded louder than it should have. More than once, I paused, taking it in, already picturing Matthew and Cora running ahead of us while Evy tried to keep them from veering off the path. I caught myself reaching for my phone more than once, wishing I had something better to capture it with. A camera, maybe. Something worth using. The thought stuck with me longer than I expected.

Tuesday night, I reminded Evy that I still wanted to take the twins for part of the day. She hesitated, like I knew she would, so I showed her the schedule I'd put together. Every hour accounted for, every stop planned out. She looked it over, then looked at me, and finally gave in with a reluctant nod. The next morning, I picked them up right after breakfast and loaded them into the car.

The park was first. I let them run until their energy burned off in bursts, chasing each other across the grass and climbing everything they could reach. By the time they were dragging their feet back toward me, both of them were asking for food. That had been the idea. I took them to a frozen yogurt place and let them build their own parfaits. It turned messy fast, but they loved it. More importantly, they ate every bite.

By the time we made it to the grocery store, they were full, slower, easier to manage. We worked our way through the list aisle by aisle, and for a while, I thought I'd pulled it off perfectly. No grabbing, no meltdowns, no scenes. Just two tired kids and a cart that filled exactly the way it was supposed to.

The meltdown came anyway.

It hit the second we got in the car. Both of them at once. Crying hard enough that I couldn't make out words, just noise. I tried everything I could think of: talking, distracting, even turning around at a red light, but nothing touched it. By the time I pulled into the daycare parking lot, I was already bracing myself to admit defeat.

Then it stopped. Just like that.

I glanced back to check on them, expecting more tears, and found both of them slumped in their seats, fast asleep. I let out a breath I hadn't realized I'd been holding, shifted the car into reverse, and backed slowly out of the lot. When I pulled into Evy's driveway, I left the engine off and moved as quietly as I could, unloading the groceries one bag at a time while they slept in the back seat, completely unaware of the chaos they'd left behind.

I went back to the daycare center to drop off the children, as arranged, after I had put the groceries away. Just as I parked, I heard the sounds of waking up coming from the back seat.

"We see Mommy now?" asked Cora.

"I hungry," said Matthew.

I unhooked them from their child seats and led the two into the building, silently congratulating myself on a good showing. Evy would never know how close I'd come to crying myself.

The next day, Evy had parent-teacher conferences, so she asked me to pick up Matthew and Cora from daycare and bring them home for lunch. She usually kept them for half a day on conference days and had her mom take over after, but this time she handed it off to me. When I arrived, both kids came barreling toward me the second they saw me, already talking over each other before I even got them out the door.

"Food now?" Matthew asked, tugging at my hand.

"I pick!" Cora added, bouncing on her toes.

I hesitated for half a second, then gave in. "All right. You pick."

They led me straight to a fast-food place with a play area, a place they'd obviously been to many times before. Lunch turned into a blur of napkins, spilled drinks, and repeated reminders to sit down and eat something that wasn't just fries. Every time I thought we were done, one of them would jump up and disappear toward the play structure again, only to come racing back a minute later, breathless and laughing.

By the time I finally got them back into their seats, both of them had slowed, their voices quieter, their movements less frantic. It didn't take long after that. The drive home was silent.

When I pulled into the driveway, I glanced in the rearview mirror and found both of them asleep, heads tilted at impossible angles, mouths slightly open. I sat there for a second, engine off, listening to the quiet settle around us, feeling it catch up to me all at once.

Inside, I carried them in one at a time, careful not to wake them. Shoes off. Socks peeled away. Clothes dropped into the hamper. They barely stirred as I tucked them into their beds, each of them curling instinctively into the mattress as if we'd done it a hundred times before.

When I finally made it back to the living room, I sank onto the couch, telling myself I'd just rest for a minute. Just a minute.

The next thing I knew, everything had gone dark.

Evy

I walked into the house to see Henry sprawled out asleep on my couch. I put a hand over my mouth to stifle the laughter. The couple of hours with the twins must've worn him out. He hadn't even taken his knit cap off, and it was now askew, making him look all the more mussed and raggedy. I walked over and gently removed the cap without waking him up. Obviously, he needed the rest after dealing with my twosome. Then I gasped as I realized his hair was growing out and he was looking more like 'Ace.'

I paused in the doorway long enough to make sure Matthew and Cora were still asleep, both of them curled into their blankets without stirring. Satisfied, I pulled the door mostly closed and headed into the kitchen. The quiet felt different after the chaos of the day. I moved through the motions automatically, pulling ingredients from the fridge, layering everything into a dish, sliding it into the oven. The timer clicked into place, the soft hum filling the space where noise had been only minutes before.

I leaned my hands against the counter for a moment, staring at nothing in particular.

It had been a week.

The thought settled in slowly, heavier than it should have. A week since Henry had asked to move in. He hadn't mentioned it again, not once, giving me space or waiting for me to bring it up. But I hadn't forgotten. There hadn't been a single moment I hadn't been aware of it, sitting there in the background of everything else.

I pushed off the counter and crossed my arms loosely, shifting my weight from one foot to the other. The answer itself didn't scare me. That part felt easy. What didn't feel easy was everything that came with it. This wasn't just me. It couldn't be.

My gaze drifted toward the hallway, toward the room where the twins slept, the house suddenly feeling quieter because of it.

I drew in a slow breath.

If he was going to be part of our life, then he had to be part of theirs too.

Just as I thought this, I heard them stirring in their room. I walked to their room and shut the door. I held a finger up to my lips, showing they should be quiet. They looked at me wide-eyed.

"Henry is asleep in the living room," I explained as I sat on Cora's bed. My daughter snuggled up next to me.

Both Matthew and Cora giggled, and I smiled.

"I have a very important question for you," I said to them. "Henry is very nice, don't you agree?"

Matthew and Cora nodded in unison at me. I had often remarked that they did this, even though they were only fraternal twins.

"I like Henry very much. He's my boyfriend. Do you know what a boyfriend is?" I asked.

Matthew looked at me curiously with his blue eyes, so like mine. "No."

Cora asked, "Is that boy that is friend?"

"Sort of," I said. "It's a boy who is a friend that you love."

"Ooooh," replied Cora.

"I'd like to ask Henry to move into our house and live with us. But only if it's okay with the two of you," I explained.

Matthew asked, "Where he sleep? On couch? Like now? He too big for my bed."

"No, baby. He would sleep in my room," I replied, laughing. I reached over to ruffle my son's brown hair.

With a tilt of his head, Matthew contemplated this answer. "I thought you said mommies and daddies sleep in same room."

"Yes, that's usually true. But sometimes a man and a woman who love each other sleep in the same room."

Cora looked at me. "Henry make Mommy happy?"

"Yes, baby, he does," I said with a sheen of tears in my eyes.

Cora hugged me. "He stay."

Not to be left out, Matthew clambered off his own toddler bed to join the hug and said, "Okay!"

I embraced my children while silent tears slid down my cheeks. I let them go and surreptitiously wiped the wetness away. "Let's go wake him up and tell him our news."

HENRY

Upon waking, I quickly realized that I'd fallen asleep on the couch at Evy's. My first clue was the little hand that was poking me in the nose and saying, "Wake up." I waved the hand away, recognizing Matthew's voice. "Matthew, stop that, please."

I opened my eyes to see not only Matthew, but Cora and Evy all looking at me. Evy was trying not to laugh as Cora stood between my legs, holding a pillow over her head, ready to pummel me with it. Her brown eyes twinkled devilishly, and her brown hair, wild and unbrushed since her nap, enhanced the look. I quickly put my hands up to protect myself from the onslaught. "Why am I under attack?"

"That's what can happen when you fall asleep with two three-year-olds around," laughed Evy.

"Mommy said wake Henry up!" revealed Cora.

Matthew said, "Tell Henry stay!"

Surprised by this last set of words, I put my hands down, thinking I must have misunderstood. "What?"

Cora took that cue to mean she could launch her attack and hit me square in the face with the pillow. Stunned by what had been said previously, I hadn't even tried to block the assault. My eyes closed in reflex and lay there.

"Henry, okay?" Cora said in shock when I didn't move.

I sat up and answered, "I'm okay, Cora."

I ruffled her hair, and she smiled, reassured by my words. I swung my legs off the couch and looked at Matthew.

"What did you say before?" I asked him.

"Momma said tell you stay," he told me.

I hadn't heard wrong. Looking towards Evy, she grinned and nodded at the question in my eyes. Her look also promised that we would discuss this more later.

"Kids, let's go clean up, then you can play until dinner time. The three of you slept longer than expected," she said, shooing the twins towards the bathroom so she could make sure they washed their faces and hands.

Once the twins settled down after their ambush, the evening slipped into its usual rhythm. Dinner was noisy, baths even more so, and by the time Matthew and Cora were finally tucked into bed, the house felt like it had exhaled. The quiet that followed rang in my ears.

Evy and I lingered in the living room for a moment, neither of us sitting down right away. I glanced toward the hallway, then back at her.

"I should go grab my things," I said, already reaching for my keys. "It won't take long."

She shook her head before I could move. "Not tonight."

I paused, caught halfway between standing and staying. "Why not?"

Evy stepped closer, lowering her voice even though the twins were already asleep. "Because they'll wake up tomorrow and you'll just be here. That's a lot for them all at once."

I hesitated, the urgency still there, pressing at me. I wanted my things here. I wanted to be here. Not halfway in, not waiting.

"I just..." I ran a hand through my hair, exhaling. "I don't want to leave again."

Her expression softened, and she reached for my hand, threading her fingers through mine. "You're not leaving. You're just waiting until morning."

I looked at her for a second longer, then let out a breath and nodded.

Morning suddenly felt a lot farther away than it should have.

"But, honey," she said, placing her hand on my thigh, "With the twins asleep, there is nothing stopping us from having some time alone."

Evy stood up and led me from the living room to her bedroom. Fortunately, the design of the house meant the bathroom was between her room and the twins'. She shut the door, but when she went to turn on the light, I stopped her. "Leave it off," I said as I opened the curtains instead.

Moonlight filled the room with its soft glow. I sat on the bed and beckoned Evy to stand in front of me. Slowly, I unbuttoned the shirt she had on and eased it off her shoulders. I buried my face in her cleavage, taking a deep breath. Evy held my head against her briefly, then reached behind her to undo and remove her bra. Next, she hauled the polo shirt over my head so she could feel my skin on hers. Time apart had caused me to miss the smell, the taste, the feel of her. She leaned forward to nip my shoulder. I must taste faintly salty as she soothed the spot she'd bitten with a slow sweep of her tongue.

I groaned and leaned forward to take her nipple in my mouth. Evy's head fell backward as I sucked, licked, and bit at the tip of her breast. Too soon I released it, but then gave my attention to the other one.

The two of us took our time with this lovemaking, reacquainting ourselves with each other's bodies. We also knew that we had to be aware of the sleeping children in the house two doors away. Kisses had to be muffled, or else we caught our moans, sounds, and words of love.

When we finally came together again after nearly two weeks apart, I told her I loved her—first with words, then with the way I touched her. I slid into her slowly, my gaze locked on hers.

She gasped, whispered, "I love you," and pulled me closer, begging me to go deeper.

In the quiet afterward, Evy curled into me, fitting against my chest as if she belonged there. My arms settled around her waist, holding her in place as if I could keep the moment from shifting. She didn't move right away, just stayed there, her fingers lightly gripping my forearm, like letting go wasn't something she was ready to do.

I pressed my face into her hair and closed my eyes. If I didn't move, maybe the night wouldn't end.

For a while, neither of us said anything.

Then she shifted in my arms, just enough to turn toward me. Her hand slid up to my chest, resting there, and I felt the hesitation before she spoke.

"Henry... it's time for you to go."

I didn't answer right away. I tightened my hold on her instead, my chin brushing the top of her head.

"I know," I said finally, though I made no move to let her go.

She tilted her face up to mine, her expression soft in the low light. "It's only a few more hours," she whispered. "Tomorrow you'll be here."

I nodded, more to myself than to her, then leaned in and kissed her, slower this time, like

I was trying to hold on to something that was already slipping away.

When I pulled back, I stayed there for a second longer before forcing myself to sit up. The air felt colder the moment I left the bed. I dressed without rushing, aware of her watching me, even without looking.

At the door, I paused, my hand on the handle, and glanced back at her. "Good night, sweetheart."

I stepped into the hallway before I could change my mind.

"Henry."

I turned too quickly, hope rising before I could stop it. "Yeah?"

She crossed the room and held out my keys and wallet, a small smile touching her lips. "You probably don't want to forget these."

I let out a quiet breath and took them from her, my fingers brushing hers for just a second longer than necessary.

"Right," I said softly.

Chapter 8

EVY

I had just finished making breakfast for the twins and me when a knock sounded at the door. I wiped my hands on a towel and went to answer it.

Henry stood on the other side with a grin and two suitcases at his feet.

Before I could say a word, Matthew and Cora rushed past me.

"Can we take your stuff?" Cora asked, already reaching for one of the handles.

Henry blinked at her, clearly thrown for a second, then glanced down at the bags and laughed. "My stuff, huh? Yeah. Go ahead."

They grabbed the suitcases and dragged them down the hallway, bumping into the wall more than once as they disappeared from view.

Henry watched them go, then slowly turned his head toward me.

I was already laughing.

"You think that's funny?" he asked, starting toward me.

I backed up, still smiling, not nearly fast enough to escape him. He caught me easily, pressing me between the chair and his body, one hand braced on the backrest.

"The twins could come back any second," I whispered, though I made no move to slip away.

His gaze flicked toward the hallway, then back to me. "Fine," he mumbled. "But don't think I'm letting this go."

I held his gaze for a second longer before stepping around him, picking up the towel again like I needed something to do with my hands.

"I'll clean up breakfast," I said. "You might want to go find your things before they disappear completely."

Later, hearing giggles, I walked out of the kitchen to see Cora standing on the couch with the doll that Henry had given her, while Matthew was on the floor with his robot. Henry had one of the twin's handmade capes on. He knelt on the floor next to Matthew with a stick in his hand, holding it like a staff.

"As long as I stand, you're safe," Henry said in a deeper voice.

I recognized it as the line that his character, Vigil Warden, said when saving people from the most dangerous situations in each movie. Here, Cora and her doll were the ones being saved from her brother and his robot. Their play and Henry joining in made me start to laugh. Henry heard me and glanced toward me.

Suddenly I stopped laughing, and he watched my look change to surprise. I gaped behind him at the front door of the house, which had just opened, but we had not heard it. It was warmer today, and we'd also opened the windows to allow the breeze in.

Henry rotated around from his place on the floor to see my mother and aunt standing in the doorway staring at him. They both screamed, but this was a fan scream. They had apparently heard him say the lines from the movie in his Vigil Warden voice. It had caused them to realize who he was, despite the minor changes to his appearance.

I ran to the door and yanked both women into the house before slamming it shut. I then leaned against it and looked at him with a question on my face, silently asking him how to handle this. It was exactly what we'd wanted to avoid.

After assuring the children that the women were fine, the twins went to their room to play. Maeve, Eileen, Henry and I all sat down in the living area to have a heart to heart. The older women sat on one side of the couch while Henry was at the opposite end. I sat on the armrest next to him. We hoped that there was a way to convince the women to keep his secret. It was the only way we could maintain our relationship.

"You're Ace Starling!" cried Aunt Eileen.

"Yes and no," Henry said, both leaning back and putting up his hands towards the two women. "My name is Henry Starling, but my stage name is Ace Starling. I'm the same person I was yesterday. I'm also an actor who makes famous movies."

"But why have you been hiding it?" asked my mother. Both women crowded in around Henry.

"Because of the reaction you just had," replied Henry. "I can't have a real life because of being famous. Though I haven't been hiding. I told you my real name; I just left out my stage name. "

"You've known about this all along?" asked Mom, looking towards me with dismay. She was in disbelief that I would keep something like this from her.

I wanted to put myself between my family and Henry, but refrained. I said in apology, "Yes,

Mom. But I knew you would act exactly like this. Plus, as a lifelong resident of Belding and the main credit union bank teller ..."

"Semi-retired bank teller," my mother corrected.

I went on. "Fine, as the main credit union semi-retired bank teller, you know almost everyone in town! I couldn't trust you with this type of information."

"I want to live here with Evy and the twins as much as my schedule allows. To do this, I have to ask both of you to keep my secret for a little longer. Will you do this for us?" he asked my mother and aunt.

The two women looked at each other with similar pained expressions. They loved to gossip, and this was the biggest story to hit their small town in years! Aunt Eileen spun back towards us first. "Yes, of course. Right, Maeve?"

Eileen pivoted to look at Mom and nudged her with her elbow. "Yes, yes. Of course!" she said. "Though if we can be the ones to tell others eventually, that'd be great."

"Mom!" I exclaimed in disbelief, rolling my eyes.

Henry laughed, "We'll see what we can do, Maeve."

"Now, though, young man, I have to ask what your intentions toward my daughter are. You've seen we are church-going people," said my mom, crossing her arms over her chest and looking at him over her glasses.

I glared at my mother. "This from the person who cheats at cards in the church hall."

Maeve put on a look of innocence. "I do not cheat; I even the odds."

"I assure you, I love your daughter; marriage is most likely in our future. We have to wait until we understand our relationship better. My schedule will be a big enough issue to work around everything else."

I peeked a glance at him. We hadn't talked about marriage. This was the first time he had mentioned it. Warmth began in my chest at the mental image of being married to Henry. He caught me eyeing him and squeezed my hand.

Both Eileen and Mom nodded and smiled at his answer, obviously satisfied, but they leaned forward as one and spoke in rapid fire, "So how much dish can you give us about the other celebrities? Which ones do you know really well? Can you introduce us to any?" The questions flew at Henry from both of them.

Henry's mouth dropped open, and I quickly took my mother and aunt by the arms, lifting them out of the seats and leading them to the door. "Out, you gossipmongers! My boyfriend's not here to give you the celebrity scoop."

"But Evy..." started my mom.

"Nope, nada, never," I said, letting go of the two as I pushed them through the doorway. "This is why we kept Henry's identity hidden. We didn't want people bothering him because of his connections. My own family doing so is the worst!"

I shut the door in the two women's faces, then walked back to the kitchen where Henry still stood in shock. What I had done had happened so fast, he had barely moved. I looked at Henry, and we both started laughing. "Are you sure this is still what you want, honey?" I asked him. "My family comes along with me…"

Henry

The first few mornings, I woke before everyone else out of habit. The house was quiet then, the kind of quiet I wasn't used to anymore, and I found myself moving around the kitchen carefully, like I didn't quite belong there yet. By the end of the week, that had changed. One morning Matthew dragged a chair over to "help" stir pancake batter, on another Cora insisted on choosing what went on her plate, and somehow I learned how to manage both without burning anything. It became routine before I realized it had.

The rest of the days filled in around that. Some mornings I kept the twins home, loading them into the car with half a plan and figuring out the rest as we went. Other days I ran errands, moving through the grocery store with a list Evy had written, catching myself adding things I knew she liked without thinking about it. A couple of times a week, I stepped outside that life just long enough to call Erik, pacing in the yard or sitting in my car while we talked through contracts and schedules. Those calls felt shorter each time, like I was rushing to get back to something that mattered more.

Around town, people started recognizing me, not for who I was, but for where I fit. A nod from across the street. A cashier asking how "the kids" were doing. It was different from New York, where I was either invisible or watched too closely. Here, I was just... there. Part of it.

Evenings settled into something steady. Dinner at the table, the twins talking over each other while Evy tried to keep them on track, then baths, bedtime, and finally the quiet that followed. We'd end up on the couch or side by side with a book, not always talking, but not needing to. It felt easy in a way I hadn't expected. Natural.

Jonathan and his daughter came by a couple of times, and I got used to the rhythm of that too. The kids disappeared into their own world almost immediately, leaving the rest of us to sit and talk. I learned pieces of their history in between stories and laughter, enough to understand how firmly Evy was rooted here, how much of her life was tied to the people around her. It made what we were building feel less temporary.

Vincent showed up once. Just once.

He stayed long enough to take the twins out, long enough for me to see the distance there, then he was gone again with an excuse that didn't quite land. I didn't ask questions, but I watched Evy after he left, the way she brushed it off like it was normal.

I didn't understand it. I wasn't sure I ever would.

What I understood was how easily I'd slipped into all of this. The house. The routines. The kids. Evy. It stopped feeling like something I was stepping into and started feeling like something that was mine.

Which was probably why I didn't see it coming when the other part of my life pushed its way back in.

I was on the phone with Erik, half-listening as he ran through details about the next film, when he said, "So when are you coming back for the gala? It's in four days."

I went still.

The gala.

I closed my eyes and dragged a hand down my face. I'd completely lost track of it.

"I'll be there," I said, already feeling the weight of it settle in. "I'll be there. Send the jet to a nearby airport and also arrange for a hangar rental there," I replied.

"Will do. I'll text you about which airport it will be. Which suit do you want me to get ready for you then?" asked Erik.

I told him before hanging up, "The blue tuxedo with the black lapels."

I'd have to talk to Evy about it tonight and leave two days after tomorrow. And plan to be gone for three days. I ran a hand over my face again. We hadn't talked about my leaving since the first day I'd arrived and had mentioned I had three weeks until I had a commitment. I sighed and leaned my head against the back of the couch. Why did it make me feel so devastated to have to leave for a few days?

Evy

When I walked into the house with Matthew and Cora, I found Henry on the couch. He was leaning forward, elbows on his thighs, his hands hanging loosely between them. His head rested back against the cushion, as if even holding it up had become too much.

I didn't need to ask to know something was wrong.

"Let's go see Gramma," I said lightly, turning the twins back toward the door before they could start asking questions.

They went without protest, and after a quick explanation to my mom, I slipped back into the house alone.

Henry hadn't moved.

I crossed the room and sat beside him, reaching for one of his hands and holding it between both of mine. "Henry? Hon… what's wrong?"

He turned his head toward me, then pushed himself upright with a small shake of it. "Sorry. I didn't mean to worry you."

I waited.

"I forgot about something," he said after a moment. "An event. I have to go back to New York for it. It's in four days."

"Oh," I breathed, the tightness in my chest easing just a little, though it didn't go away completely.

"I'll only be gone a few days," he added quickly. "Three, maybe. Then I'm back here for a while."

I nodded, absorbing that, then shifted closer when his arm came around my shoulders. I leaned into him, feeling the tension still sitting in his body.

"Tell me about it," I said quietly.

He was silent for a moment, like he was deciding how much to say.

"It's a gala," he said finally. "For a charity I helped start. It benefits foster children. I go every year."

His thumb brushed absently along my arm as he spoke.

"I had neighbors growing up who took in foster kids. I watched them struggle. But they loved those children and helped them so much. I started it with the actress who was the original love interest in the first two Vigil Warden movies, Rachael Westfield. She and I discovered we shared a common interest in supporting foster kids."

He paused before continuing.

"I used to care about it more. About being there. Now it just..." He exhaled softly. "Feels like something I have to show up for."

I tilted my head back to look at him. "What changed?"

He hesitated, then answered more quietly. "The person I started it with. We're not... close anymore."

I didn't push, just watched him, letting him decide what to give me.

"She thought I had something to do with her being cut from the film," he said. "I didn't. But it didn't matter."

The silence that followed felt heavier than his words.

"I still care about the charity," he went on. "Just not the rest of it."

I shifted slightly, sliding my hand over his chest. "Then go for that part," I said softly. "The part that still matters."

His arm tightened around me, and he pressed a kiss to my temple.

"I'm going to miss you," he murmured.

I closed my eyes for a second, letting that settle.

"We'll still be here when you get back."

HENRY

I stood off to the side of the hotel ballroom, sipping my champagne. I peered out over the crowded room, seeming to others that I was interested in who was in attendance, but in reality my heart was in a small town in Michigan with an auburn-haired woman and her two children. Glancing at my watch, I realized Evy was probably putting the twins to bed right now. My heart ached that I was missing the nightly ritual. It had become so important to me in such a short time.

Out of the corner of my eye, I saw a woman sidling up to me. She wore a coral-colored, one-shoulder cocktail dress with a gold belt. Her gold high heels placed her almost at eye level with me. She reached out and slid her hand up the sleeve of my blue tuxedoed arm.

"Ace, darling, why are you hiding over here all by yourself?"

I reached out and brushed off her hand, and stepped away. "Go away, Chloe."

"Now, that's no way to talk to me when we were once together." She pouted her red-rouged lips, batting her heavily mascaraed eyes as she brushed her cascading chestnut-brown hair behind her shoulder in what she must've believed was a sexy move.

With a harsh laugh that must've stung, I asked, "Together, is that what you call two dates several *years* ago?" The emphasis on the word 'years' was clear.

At that, Chloe flounced away, tossing over her shoulder, "Enjoy this party alone then. No wonder you're still single and standing by yourself in a corner."

Chloe was an example of exactly the type of person who attended the gala dinner. When I first became famous, I'd considered this crowd to be exciting, but their shallowness had worn thin quickly. I no longer enjoyed spending time with most of the rich and famous, who only wanted to party and spend money to show that they had nothing else to do. At least they donated money to the charity and came to the gala since it was a society news feature.

I scanned the crowd again and found Erik over by the bar. Setting down my champagne glass on a passing server's tray, I walked over to him and announced. "I'm leaving."

Erik regarded me and knew better than to argue. "I'd recommend letting your co-chair know that you are leaving early. It'd be the polite thing to do."

"Do you think she cares about what I do?" I queried, rolling my eyes. Then I grumbled resignedly, "Fine, I'll find her and let her know."

I turned and surveyed the crowded ballroom once again. I saw Rachael surrounded by an entourage, like a queen at court. She still took pleasure in the gala, at least as much as I used to. I wove my way through the crowd until I was next to her, though she'd yet to see me. "Rachael, may I speak with you?"

Spinning quickly towards me, Rachael switched from laughing in enjoyment to having a neutral, almost disgusted look directed at me. The misunderstanding still pained me, as it had destroyed our friendship. She eyed me with disinterest. "Go ahead, talk."

"I wanted to let you know I'm leaving the gala early," I retorted, almost instantly biting back the tone I really wanted to use.

"And why does that matter to me?" Rachael glanced at her companions, laughing to show them how little she thought of me. It was her way of saving face after our fallout. And it worked.

I gritted my teeth as she was obviously trying to belittle me. "As co-chair of the gala, I figured it was the polite thing to do."

Rachael waved her hand in dismissal. "Fine, go then."

Giving a slight bow, I announced to the entire group, "Goodnight and enjoy yourselves. Thank you for attending the gala and supporting the charity."

As I strode away, I missed Rachael pivoting her head slightly towards me with a momentary look of concern on her face. This was the first time I'd ever left the gala early in all the years of the event. I walked back to Erik and told him to have the jet ready to go in the morning. There was nothing of importance keeping me in New York, so why stay the extra day I'd originally planned? I felt I'd need to take a day to recover, but since I was now leaving the event and arriving back at my penthouse well before midnight...

Erik gave me a sideways look but just said, "Yes, boss," as he watched me turn and leave the ballroom. As I exited the ballroom doors, anyone watching would've believed I had an emergency with the speed that I left.

Chapter 9

Evy

On the third day Henry was gone, I took the twins to the mall in the next town over. They had outgrown nearly everything again, shoes and pants most of all, and I was still trying to figure out how that kept happening so fast. Before we left, I called Jonathan to see if he and Geneva wanted to come along. Shopping would be easier with another adult, and I could use the company.

Jonathan pulled up in his minivan, and within minutes the kids were climbing in, already talking over each other. By the time we reached the mall, we headed straight for the food court, making sure everyone was fed before attempting anything else.

Shopping with three small kids meant moving in bursts. One minute we were weaving through racks, the next we were waiting outside dressing rooms, counting heads every few seconds to make sure no one had wandered off. Somewhere in between grabbing sizes and chasing after Cora, Jonathan asked how Mallorca had been. That was all it took.

The story came out in pieces at first. Meeting Henry. The island. Him showing up at my house. Everything that had happened since. Jonathan interrupted little, just asked the occasional question and let me talk, like he knew I needed to get it out more than I needed advice.

By the time we ended up in the play area, the kids had disappeared into their own world, and the two of us finally had a chance to sit.

Jonathan leaned back in his chair, watching Geneva climb the structure before looking at me. "You've already made your decision, you know."

I frowned slightly. "Have I?"

"You let him move in. You gave him a key. He's taking the twins a couple of days a week." He shrugged. "Sounds like settling down to me."

I looked down at my hands, rubbing my thumb along the edge of the table. He wasn't wrong.

"I love him," I said quietly. "I do. And he says he loves me." I hesitated, searching for the right words. "It's just... fast. Everything about this is fast. And I keep waiting for something to go wrong."

Jonathan tapped his finger lightly against the table. "Fast doesn't mean wrong."

I glanced up at him.

"You were with Vincent for years," he went on. "That didn't make it right either."

I let out a small breath at that, not quite a laugh.

"This feels different," I admitted. "Too good, maybe."

He studied me for a second longer, then asked, "What aren't you saying?"

I hesitated, then looked back down at my hands again.

"He didn't ask me to go with him," I said. "To the gala."

Jonathan didn't speak, so I kept going.

"He said he didn't want to pull me into that part of his life yet." I swallowed. "I didn't think it bothered me, but... it does."

I twisted my fingers together in my lap. "What if there's someone else? Or he doesn't want to be seen with me?"

Jonathan reached across the table and stilled my hands with his.

"You're overthinking this," he said gently. "Anyone with eyes can see how he looks at you. That man is in love with you."

I didn't answer right away.

"The only way you're going to know," he added, "is to ask him."

I nodded slowly, even though the thought of doing that made my stomach tighten.

Knowing what to do and actually doing it were two very different things.

HENRY

When I arrived at the little house I now considered my home, I didn't expect it to be empty, as Evy's car was out front. Immediately, I felt disappointed, but realized I should've contacted Evy to let her know I was coming back earlier than expected. I'd been there for about an hour and was trying to decide if I should start dinner when I heard car doors closing along with lots of laughter. I headed from the be kitchen to the front of the house and looked out the living room window to see Evy, the twins, Jonathan, and Geneva heading to the house. Evy immediately saw my car next to hers and broke into a run for the house, surprising the others who were with her. She called back behind her, "Henry is back!"

I heard her yell and opened the front door with a huge smile on my face to catch her as she ran in. We hugged tightly, and soon two more sets of arms hugged us around the knees. I felt my heart warm, knowing they had missed me as much as I had missed them. I laughed as I bent down and hugged both Matthew and Cora.

"I missed you so much!" I said.

"Did you bring gift?" asked Cora.

"Coralynn Mae, that is not a polite thing to ask. And Henry doesn't have to bring you a gift every time he comes back," Evy chastised her daughter, who gave her a pout in return.

I chuckled and kneeled in front of the little girl. "No, I didn't. I was in too much of a hurry to come back because I wanted to see you again. You were much more important to me than going to buy a present. I got up bright and early to pack my suitcase and get on the plane so I could come home."

By this time, Jonathan had also made it to the front door with Geneva in tow, his hands full. He had collected all the shopping bags from his minivan. I reached out and helped take some from him. "What've you all been up to?" I inquired as I peeked into the various sacks.

"The twins needed new shoes and pants, so we went over to the mall to get some. I asked Jonathan and Geneva to join us. We had lunch too," explained Evy.

"See?" said Cora, twisting her foot from side to side to show me the shoes she was wearing. They were white with unicorns on the side that had a shiny mane and horn, along with pink soles.

Not to be outdone by his sister, Matthew stomped his feet so his shoes lit up with green flashes and said, "Look! Lights!"

I laughed and admired the twins' shoes, telling them both how great they were. I had missed these simple moments with the kids.

After putting the kids down for the night, I headed back to the kitchen and found Evy already sitting at the table. She didn't look up right away. Her hands were clasped together in her lap, fingers twisting against each other.

I slowed; something in my chest tightened.

I took the chair across from her. "Evy... what's wrong?"

She bit her lip, then drew in a breath, and finally met my eyes. "I want to talk about the gala."

I nodded, waiting.

"Why didn't you ask me to go?" she asked, her voice quieter now. "Are you ashamed of me?" The words came faster after that. "Was there someone else you wanted to see?"

For a second, I just stared at her.

Then I pushed my chair back and stood, crossing the space between us. "Hey," I said softly, pulling her to her feet. "No. None of that."

She didn't relax right away.

I kept my hands on her arms, forcing her to look at me. "I love you," I said, more firmly this time. "There isn't anyone else."

Her eyes searched mine, as if she was trying to decide whether to believe me.

"I didn't ask you to come because I didn't think you'd like it," I went on, quieter now. "I didn't even want to be there; I left early."

That made her pause.

"It's not the part of my life I want you stepping into first," I added. "Not like that."

Her shoulders eased just a little, but she still looked uncertain.

Lifting a hand, I brushed it along her cheek. "I should have asked," I said. "I didn't think about how it would feel on your end."

That was the first moment she softened.

"I'm not ashamed of you," I continued, holding her gaze. "You and the twins... this is what matters to me. This is home."

She let out a breath, her body finally leaning into mine instead of holding back. I wrapped my arms around her, and this time she didn't hesitate to hold on.

For a while, neither of us spoke.

The next day, while the twins napped, I stretched out on the couch with the script the producer had sent over. I skimmed through the opening scenes, making a few mental notes as I went, the pages shifting under my thumb as I worked my way through.

I was halfway in when the front door opened.

I glanced up, already pushing myself to my feet. Evy stepped inside, earlier than usual, her bag slipping from her shoulder as she shut the door behind her.

"You're home early," I said, crossing to her. I leaned in to kiss her, but she only half-met me, her attention somewhere else.

"Are you okay?" I asked, searching her face.

"Just… give me a minute," she said, her voice trailing off as she moved past me. "I need to freshen up."

I watched her disappear down the hallway, the bathroom door closing a second later.

For a moment, I stayed where I was. Then I glanced at the clock. An hour early.

I picked the script back up, but the words blurred together. After a few seconds, I dropped it onto the couch beside me and leaned forward, elbows on my knees, listening to the faint sounds from the other room.

Something wasn't right.

A few minutes later, Evy came back and sat down beside me, her face still damp from washing it. She didn't look at me right away, just stared down at her hands, twisting her fingers together in her lap.

"I… don't know where to start," she said quietly.

I reached over and took one of her hands, running my thumb across her knuckles. "Take your time."

She nodded once, then drew a breath. "Remember when I thought I had that stomach bug last week?"

I nodded.

"It wasn't that," she said. Her voice wavered just slightly before she steadied it. "I went to the doctor today."

My grip on her hand tightened. "And?"

She finally looked at me. "I'm pregnant."

For a second, the words didn't land. Then they did.

I just stared at her, my mind catching up all at once, and then something broke loose in my chest. I stood, pulling her up with me without thinking, wrapping my arms around her and lifting her off the ground.

"Henry," she laughed, breathless, "you're going to make me sick."

I set her down immediately, my hands still on her like I needed to make sure she was real. "I'm sorry," I said quickly, searching her face. "Are you okay? What do you need?"

She let out a small breath, somewhere between a laugh and something else. "I'm okay."

I exhaled, the tension leaving me all at once. "Five weeks?" I asked, quieter now.

She nodded. "About that."

I dropped to my knees in front of her before I could think better of it, resting my cheek lightly against her stomach. "Mallorca?" I asked, my voice softer than I'd ever heard it.

"Yes," she said, her fingers slipping into my hair.

For a moment, I just stayed there.

Then I leaned back, looking up at her, and the smile that broke across my face felt impossible to hold in. "We're having a baby," I said, almost to myself.

Her eyes filled, and I saw the uncertainty there before she could hide it.

I pushed to my feet and cupped her face in my hands. "Hey," I said gently. "This is good. This is... more than good."

She searched my face as if she was still trying to find the truth in it.

"I mean that," I added quietly.

I hesitated for just a second, then nodded to myself.

"Stay here," I said, holding up a finger before stepping away.

I crossed into the bedroom, reached into the drawer where I'd hidden it, and came back a moment later, my hand closing around the small box in my pocket.

Evy watched me carefully as I sat down in front of her again, this time slower.

"Meeting you in Mallorca..." I started, then stopped, shaking my head slightly. "I didn't expect any of this. But I knew, even then, that I didn't want to walk away from you."

I pulled the box from my pocket and opened it; the ring catching the light between us.

"So I stopped waiting for the perfect moment," I said, my voice steady now. "Because every moment with you already is one."

I took her hand in mine.

"Evy, will you marry me?"

Her breath caught, her eyes dropping to the ring, then lifting back to mine. "Henry... have you been carrying that around since..."

I smiled slightly. "Mallorca."

She let out a soft, disbelieving laugh, her hand coming up to her mouth before she lowered it again.

"Yes," she said, her voice breaking into a smile. "Yes, of course I will."

She leaned forward, her hands framing my face as she kissed me, and I slid the ring onto her finger before pulling her closer again. The moment settled around us in a way that felt like it might finally hold.

I leaned forward to kiss her again, and then deepened the kiss. As I did so, we both heard giggles coming from behind us. Spinning, we saw the twins standing in their open bedroom doorway, now awake from their nap. "Come here, you two," said Evy.

The four of us settled onto the couch, the twins pressed in close on either side of us, their attention locked on Evy's hand.

"What that?" Cora asked, reaching for the ring.

"It means Henry asked me to marry him," Evy said gently. "And I said yes."

Matthew frowned slightly. "Marry?"

"It means we're going to be a family," I said, keeping my voice simple. "All of us."

They both looked at me, then back at Evy, then at each other, as if they were trying to piece it together.

"You Daddy now?" Matthew asked.

Evy and I exchanged a quick glance.

"You already have a dad," she said carefully. "Vincent will always be your dad."

I leaned forward a little, meeting their eyes. "But I can be here too," I added. "I can take care of you, help you, be with you."

Cora tilted her head. "Two daddies?"

"Two daddies," Evy confirmed.

They seemed to consider that for a moment, then both nodded like that made perfect sense.

"Tell Gramma?" Cora asked suddenly, bouncing a little where she sat.

"And Aunt Eileen?" Matthew added.

Evy laughed softly, looking over at me. I nodded.

"Yeah," she said. "I think we can do that."

The twins were already halfway off the couch before she finished speaking.

I glanced at Evy, and she smiled back at me, something warm and steady in her expression.

"Let's go," she said.

Chapter 10

Evy

Mom and Aunt Eileen didn't even try to hide their excitement.

"A wedding," Mom said, already reaching for a notepad on the counter. "We need a date, a venue—"

"Mom," I cut in, laughing. "We just got engaged."

"That doesn't mean we can't start planning," Aunt Eileen added, already leaning over her shoulder to look at the page.

Henry chuckled beside me. "We might need to slow this down a little."

I nodded. "We haven't even talked about when yet, and his filming schedule is going to matter."

Mom sighed as if we were personally delaying her happiness, but she set the pen down. "Fine. For now."

"For now," Aunt Eileen echoed, though the look they exchanged told me this conversation wasn't over.

Later, back at the house, the energy shifted. The twins went down easier than usual, worn out from the day, and the house settled into a quiet that felt completely different from earlier.

When I climbed into bed, Henry followed, pulling me against him almost immediately.

"So," he said softly, his hand resting low on my stomach, "what happens next?"

I smiled, turning slightly so I could see his face. "You mean with the baby?"

He nodded. "Everything."

I let out a small breath, thinking it through. "I'll have an ultrasound in a few weeks. They'll want to check how everything's progressing."

He tightened his hold on me just a little. "Tell me when it is. I want to be there."

I looked at him for a second; the certainty in his voice catching me off guard in the best way.

"Okay," I said quietly.

He didn't let go, his hand still resting there as if he already belonged in that future.

"I'll go with you. As soon as you know the date, let me know so I can put it on my calendar. It takes priority over everything else," he immediately promised. It wasn't a question or a request. It was a vow.

"Of course," I replied with a smile. It thrilled me he wanted to be involved so much from the very beginning. Vincent has been so bitter about my previous pregnancy he hadn't cared at all. I lay back on the bed and reached to turn out the light.

"Oh," Henry said quietly, like he'd just remembered something. "There's something I wanted to talk to you about."

I turned toward him.

"I have a film premiere in four weeks," he continued. "I can bring someone with me." He hesitated just long enough for my stomach to tighten. "I want you to come."

I blinked at him.

"A premiere?" I repeated, like I needed to hear it again to understand it.

He nodded, watching me carefully now. "The director asked me to be there. It's important." His voice softened. "And I want to introduce you. Not just to the people there. To everyone."

I stared at him, trying to picture it. Cameras. Crowds. People who belonged in that world.

I didn't.

"I don't know if I'd fit there," I admitted, my voice quieter now.

Henry shifted closer, his hand finding mine. "You fit with me," he said simply.

That didn't answer everything, but it made something in my chest loosen.

I let out a small breath. "You're not making this easy to say no to."

"I'm not trying to," he said, a hint of a smile breaking through.

I looked at him for another second, then nodded. "Okay."

The change in him was immediate. His face lit up, and he pulled me into a tight embrace.

"Thank you," he murmured against my hair.

I held onto him, my mind already racing ahead to everything I didn't know, everything that could go wrong. But underneath it was something else, something steadier.

If he wanted me there, then I would go.

"We'll figure out the details later," I said softly.

He nodded, still holding me, as if he didn't quite want to let go.

***

The next morning, I caught myself staring at the ring again.

The light from the classroom window hit it just right, the stone catching and holding it, and for a second I forgot what I'd been doing. I turned my hand slightly, watching it shift, still not quite believing it was actually there.

Everything felt different.

Mallorca.

Henry showing up at my door.

Him moving in.

The baby.

The proposal.

And now, a film premiere.

It all stacked on top of each other until it didn't feel real anymore, like I'd stepped into someone else's life and was just waiting for it to snap back.

"Ms. Evy!"

A small hand smacked against my leg.

I blinked, the moment breaking as I looked down at Joshua, his face scrunched in frustration.

"Joshua, what've I told you about using your words to ask for help?" I chastised the little tow-headed boy who stood at my side.

Pouting, Joshua complained, "Ms. Evy, I want to play with blocks. William won't let me."

I realized I'd been in my own world and missed that my teacher assistant had left the room. During that time, one child, William, had taken all the building blocks and wasn't letting any of the other students play with them. I stood up from where I'd been sitting at my desk, originally to work on my weekly parent newsletter, to deal with the situation.

My job was something that I could always count on to bring me back to the real world. Children not only would let you know how they really conceptualized things, but they also put things into perspective. I needed to focus on my work and not my personal life, even though it kept trying to push its way to the forefront. There was no way to separate my work and personal life completely, but I needed to prioritize my students when I was at work. It was my job to keep them safe and to educate them.

After dealing with the block situation and waiting until my teacher assistant arrived back, I went back to my desk to complete the parent newsletter. Once I finished it, I realized I would have to tell parents I was pregnant in a couple of months. I would also need to let the preschool manager know so he could post for a substitute teacher.

I sat back in my chair, unconsciously placing my hand low on my stomach. More changes and things to be done.

HENRY

The next day, I called my parents to invite them to visit us at Evy's. I'd previously talked to them about meeting Evy before I'd come to Michigan the first time. They were excited to hear that they were going to get to meet her, Matthew, Cora, and everyone else they'd heard about. I invited them to come out and stay for a few days, with the engagement dinner being the day before they left. Even offered to arrange and pay for the place for them to stay. I hung up after the conversation, promising to send them the information and my private jet to pick them up.

My next call was to my brother. I extended the same invitation, but my brother, Tom, Thomas William Starling, couldn't take the time off work to come for the extended stay. I offered to send my jet to bring him either to the family dinner we were having, if he wanted to come to that, or just to the engagement dinner. He wanted to check with his wife first. He shared that they were expecting their first child. I congratulated my brother, wanting to share my news but knowing I had to wait. How exciting that my niece or nephew would be close in age to my own child! Tom mentioned that their parents already knew about his baby.

I told my brother to let me know his decision. Tom let me know he would follow up in the next couple of days. By the time Evy had arrived home, I'd set up a place for my parents to stay for four days. I let her know the plan, and that I was waiting to hear from my brother. She was excited to meet my parents and hoped that my brother and sister-in-law could come as well.

By evening, Tom had texted me and said that they could come for the engagement dinner and asked if I would set up transportation and overnight accommodations. I replied I would do that and send Tom the info. I then let Evy know that Tom and Erin would come for the engagement dinner. Evy reminded me to let her mother know, so that she had a final total of the number of people attending.

My parents, George John and Miriam Starling, arrived two days before the engagement dinner. I picked them up at the airport, then drove them back to the house where Evy was waiting with the twins.

The moment I stepped inside, something felt off.

Matthew was on the living room floor, crying, a shirt crumpled beside him. Down the hall, Evy's voice rang out. "Coralynn Mae, get out of the closet!"

I set my keys on the shelf near the door, muttered a quick "Excuse me" over my shoulder to my parents, and crossed the room in two strides. Scooping Matthew up along with the shirt, I headed straight for the twins' bedroom.

Evy stood in front of the closed closet door. She turned when I came in, her expression crumbling the second she saw me. Then she sank to the floor and covered her face.

Matthew went still in my arms, then twisted free and went straight to her, climbing into her lap and pressing his face against her.

The closet door creaked open.

Cora peeked out, wide-eyed, taking in the scene. She stepped out slowly, still only in her underwear.

"Come here," I said gently.

She crossed the room and climbed onto my lap. "Why Mommy crying?"

I glanced at Evy, then back at Cora. "She's upset," I said softly. "You weren't listening, and she wanted everything ready for when we got back."

Cora's gaze shifted past me toward the hallway. "You mom and dad here?"

I nodded. "They're here."

Cora slid off my lap and went to Evy. "I sorry, Mommy."

Evy lowered her hands, pulling both children close. "I'm sorry too," she said, her voice still thick.

I stood and grabbed the clothes Evy had laid out earlier. "Let's get dressed," I said.

We moved through it quietly. Evy helped Matthew with his shirt while I helped Cora step into hers, guiding her arms through the sleeves. Once they were dressed, I crouched beside Evy and brushed the last of the tears from her cheeks.

"Go freshen up," I murmured. "I've got them."

She nodded and slipped out of the room.

I took the twins' hands and led them down the hall.

My parents were in the kitchen, exactly where I'd left them, each with a cup in hand. They turned as we entered, their expressions softening when they saw the kids.

"Mom, Dad," I said, "these are Matthew and Cora."

The twins stayed close at first, watching, then slowly relaxed as I crouched beside them.

"If you want," I added, "you can call them Grand-dad and Granny."

That was all it took.

The twins lit up, and within seconds they were tugging my parents toward the hallway, eager to show off their room.

For the next half hour, it was a whirlwind of toys, books, and stuffed animals. I stood in the doorway for a while, watching, before finally stepping in.

"All right," I said, laughing. "Let's give them a break."

EVY

The lasagna had just come out of the oven, filling the kitchen with a rich, familiar smell. As we settled around the table, the Starlings began asking me about growing up.

"My dad passed away when I was young," I said, folding my hands lightly in my lap. "So I spent a lot of my summers with my grandparents."

"Where was that?" Miriam asked.

"Over in the Thumb," I replied. "Right on Saginaw Bay. I was in the water more often than not.

I don't even remember learning how to swim. I just always could."

"That sounds wonderful," she said, smiling.

"It was," I said softly. "My grandfather held onto a lot of Dutch traditions, and my grandmother..." I glanced down at the dish in front of us. "She's the one who taught me to cook."

Miriam took another bite and nodded approvingly. "This is delicious."

"Thank you. It's a little different from how she made it," I admitted. "We used cottage cheese and ground beef growing up. I've switched to ricotta and sausage."

Miriam laughed lightly. "Oh, I understand that. For years, our store didn't even carry things like that. I had to drive to Grand Forks or Fargo if I wanted anything different."

"I can send you the recipe," I offered. "The twins like helping me make it."

"I would love that."

I smiled, then glanced toward John. "So how far back does your family go?"

He leaned back slightly, clearly pleased by the question. "Farther than you'd think. All four of Henry's grandparents came over from England."

"All four?" I blinked.

"Close enough to the same time," he said with a shrug. "None of them were older than twenty."

"That's incredible."

"One was a mechanic. The other farmed," he continued. "Guess which one stuck."

I smiled. "I think I can guess."

"The farm passed down through the family," he said. "Eighty acres. My brothers and I worked it for years."

"You did all of it yourself?" I asked.

"Oh, yes," he said with a small chuckle. "Early mornings, long days. But about ten years ago, I leased it out to a dairy farm."

"That must have been a big change."

"It was the best decision I ever made," he said easily.

I studied him for a moment, still thinking of him as Mr. Starling in my head, even as the conversation flowed so naturally.

Henry leaned forward slightly. "I grew up working those fields," he said. "I'm glad they don't have to anymore."

John smirked. "That farm paid for your acting career."

Henry huffed out a quiet laugh, then shook his head. "It did. And everything else you both did." His tone shifted, becoming more serious now. "That's why I'd give you anything you wanted... if you'd let me."

Miriam reached over and rested her hand on his forearm. "We're doing just fine," she said gently.

I could tell this family had already had this conversation, most likely more than once, and would probably have it again. I could also see that Miriam was used to being the neutral party between Henry and John. Smiling inside, I stood up and asked, "Is everyone done with dinner? Who would like dessert? I can also make coffee and tea." This helped lighten the mood, and

Henry stood to help me clear the dishes from the table.

Chapter 11

HENRY

The next day, I picked up my parents and joined Evy with the twins at the local brunch restaurant where everyone was meeting. No one had a vehicle that would fit six people in it. When I saw this, I had the realization that we would need a bigger vehicle with another child on the way. Both Evy and I had sedans that fit five at most. The twins still sat in forward-facing car seats that took up most of the backseat of Evy's. There was no way we could fit an infant car seat as well. I made a mental note to talk to Evy about looking at minivans or SUVs once my parents left.

After brunch, the group split up. Maeve and Eileen left to finish the shopping for the engagement dinner. It would take place at a local hall later the next day. Her mother and aunt had arranged to use the space, as neither of our homes was big enough to fit everyone coming. In the morning, everyone was going to attend church and then go to lunch. I had to leave after lunch to go to the airport to pick up Tom and his wife.

With a smile, Miriam conceded. "You have a deal. I was looking forward to spending time with Matthew, Cora, and Evy anyway. And I'll see you later, right?"

"Yes, 5:30 pm is when we agreed upon?" asked Maeve.

At this, Evy and I looked at each other and then at our parents. We didn't know what was being talked about.

My father saw the confused looks and laughed. "Surprise! The four of us old fogies are going to watch the little ones tonight so the two of you can have an evening alone."

I watched Evy's mouth drop open at this, and I just started laughing. This is exactly something my parents would do. "Okay, fill us in on the details, you devils."

It took just a few minutes for the rundown. We'd keep to the afternoon plan that had been decided on the previous night. Maeve and Eileen would finish up what they needed to do for the engagement dinner while the rest of us spent time around town. Once the twins were tired, everyone would head back to the house for some downtime. We would then have time to get ready for our evening out. The 'old fogies' would watch the twins at Maeve's house, and later Eileen would take Miriam and John to their hotel later, so I wouldn't have to. Matthew and Cora would spend the night with their grandmother and great-aunt and then come home the next morning.

I whistled. "You guys really planned this all out. Exactly when did you have time to do this?"

"We've got our ways." My mother chuckled, winking at her co-conspirators.

"So be it to look a gift horse in the mouth, honey. We'd better figure out where we want to go eat dinner," suggested Evy to me.

Since arriving in Michigan, Evy and I hadn't had a night to ourselves. We'd had time alone in her room, but we hadn't been out or had the house to ourselves.

I leaned back and watched her get ready, taking longer than she needed to, but I didn't mind. The teal pants she chose had slits along the sides that drew my attention every time she moved. The silvery sheer top caught the light, the sequins and small flowers pulling my focus more than I cared to admit. She added burgundy drop earrings and gray boots, then picked up a cardigan as if she hadn't just made it impossible not to stare.

She stepped out of the bathroom wearing only a touch of mascara and lip gloss, which made her look fresh, not overdone. I was already waiting in the living room, dressed in gray slacks and a navy long-sleeved pullover with the sleeves pushed up to my elbows. A gray wool fedora sat on my head, black loafers on my feet.

I stepped forward and pressed a light kiss to her cheek, drawing in a breath before I could stop myself.

She caught it, and her eyebrow lifted as she looked at me, questioning, and I couldn't help the smile that followed.

"I've missed that perfume. It's the same one you wore in Mallorca, isn't it?" I asked her.

Evy blinked in surprise, then answered. "Yes. I didn't realize you paid attention to that."

Leaning forward, I whispered in her ear. My five o'clock shadow tickled her cheek. "I pay atten-tion to everything about you. But that scent." I sniffed again, then lightly bit her earlobe. "That smell alone can make me hard."

Blushing, Evy looked away at this admission from me. Though we loved each other and were expecting a child, she seemed easily embarrassed by physical touch and sexual talk, especially outside the bedroom. My words obviously excited her, but she didn't seem to be sure how to respond.

Reaching out my hand, I tucked hair behind her ear and let my hand slide down her cheek and neck. I heard and felt her breath catch, and saw her glance out from under her lashes at me.

"We should go before I forget about dinner and drag you right into the bedroom." I practically growled before wheeling away to grab my car keys.

We drove forty minutes to the largest nearby city to go to a local Italian *trattoria* with a famous chef. Luckily, we didn't have to wait long for a table for two, even though we didn't have a reservation. Evy had never been there before but had heard rave reviews about it for its genuine Italian cuisine. She and I shared an appetizer of *arancini* and a basket of fresh *focaccia* that was provided. I had the house lasagna while Evy had the *pappardelle* made with boar and fresh mushroom sauce. We shared bites of each other's entrees and agreed that they were equally delicious. For dessert, we had traditional *cannoli*. We were stuffed but happy when finished.

The drive back to the house gave us time to digest our food and talk about the engagement dinner the next day. Both of us had reflections about continuing what had started prior to leaving for dinner once we got home, but avoided the topic.

Pulling into the driveway, I parked the sedan and swiveled to Evy. She hadn't taken note and had opened the door.

"Evy, sweetheart, did what I say earlier bother you?" I asked.

Evy took a breath before twisting back to me. "I've never been comfortable with...sexual talk," she began. "But I was never really comfortable with Vincent overall. Maybe that will change with you. What you said didn't bother me. I didn't know how to respond."

I put my hand behind Evy's neck and drug her closer so she was leaning over the console.

"How did it make you feel to hear me say that your scent affected me that way?"

I watched as Evy tugged at one side of her lower lip with her upper teeth. She heard me moan upon seeing this, and I used my thumb to tug her lip down and dragged it across. "It made me feel..." She paused, swallowed, then began again, whispered, "excited."

EVY

At my confession, Henry moaned again and leaned forward to capture my lips in a kiss. He tugged me even closer, almost over the console before realizing what he was doing and stopping. Breaking off the kiss, he heard the harsh sound of both of our breathing.

"Let's go inside; neither of us needs to be caught making out in the car," Henry told me with a smirk. He got out of the car and hurried around to open the passenger side for me. He then lifted and carried me to the front door. I laughed at this, and he kissed me, changing the laughter to gasps. Soon the laughter returned, though, as he tried to hold me and unlock the door, which ended up being more than he could do. Finally, admitting defeat, Henry set me down to handle the lock and open the door.

Once inside, Henry quickly shut and locked the door before removing the fedora he was wearing. He tossed it to the side and his keys into the bowl before pivoting to me with a determined look on his face. I started backing away from him with a smile when I saw this, my laughter from earlier having faded to giggles.

"What do you think you're going to do now?" I asked. I bumped into the coffee table and glanced down to move around it. As I did so, Henry moved in quickly.

Catching me in his arms, Henry carried through with my backward momentum, edging us both towards the bedroom. He leaned into my neck, smelling the scent of the perfume that was just clinging there, along with the smell that was only mine.

"Do you want me to tell you?" he asked. I watched him wide-eyed, but nodded. Henry added, "I'm going to undress you, slowly. I want to bare each part of your perfect body and kiss it as I do so. Once you're naked, I'm going to go down on you while I'm still dressed. That's just to start."

As he spoke, Henry looked directly at me. He saw my mouth part, tongue lick my lips, and eyelids partly close as he revealed his desires. He could tell I was becoming more aroused.

Leaning in closer, he licked the open seam of my lips, teasing at my tongue. As he had been talking, we had backed up all the way to the open bedroom door.

"And I want the lights on for the whole thing."

HENRY

The sound of the twins' favorite cartoon blaring from the TV pulled me awake.

I blinked toward the ceiling, disoriented for a second before it registered. They were already home. Either Maeve hadn't woken us, or she'd decided to let us sleep in.

I rolled onto my side and nuzzled into Evy, who was somehow still asleep despite the noise. My arm slipped around her, drawing her closer, reluctant to let the quiet of the room go just yet.

Fragments of the night before lingered, enough to bring a slow smile to my face.

I let my hand drift to her stomach, resting there lightly. There was the faintest change beneath my palm, something I hadn't noticed before, or maybe hadn't let myself notice.

Evy shifted and rolled onto her back, her eyes opening slowly. She caught my expression almost immediately.

"What are you smiling about?" she asked, her voice still soft with sleep.

"Just thinking about last night," I said, leaning in to kiss the tip of her nose.

Her cheeks warmed, and she huffed out a quiet breath when my hand stayed where it was.

"That," I added gently, brushing my thumb along her side, "and this."

She tried to nudge my hand away, her expression somewhere between shy and amused. "Don't remind me. My pants are already getting tight. I'm going to start showing sooner this time."

I smiled, easing my hand away but not moving far. "We'll figure it out when we need to."

The noise from the TV carried down the hall again, louder this time.

"We should probably get up," I said. "Sounds like we've been discovered."

She groaned softly, pushing herself upright and reaching for her robe. I swung my legs over the side of the bed, stretching before standing.

I felt her gaze on me and glanced back over my shoulder, catching it. I grinned and gave her a quick wink before pulling on a pair of sweatpants.

"Come on," I said, heading toward the door. "Let's go face the morning."

After breakfast, I left to pick up my parents. Evy finished getting the twins ready and then put them in her car. As soon as service was over, the group didn't waste time before heading to the local burger joint that had been around for over forty years. Since Evy had been a child, it'd been tradition to go there after church. The small-town restaurant still had a salad buffet on Sundays and gave away kiddie cones for free. I had to depart right after eating to fetch my brother, Tom, and sister-in-law, Erin. It would take me at least two hours round trip to go to the airport and back and then drop them off at the hotel. They, as well as I, wanted to have time to rest before the engagement dinner.

Evy

I arrived home with the twins and was ready for a nap. I'd forgotten how tiring the first trimester of pregnancy could be. Once I put the twins down to sleep, I lay down in my own room and quickly fell asleep.

In what seemed to be no time at all, I awoke when I felt the bed move. I opened my eyes briefly to blearily see Henry join me. He whispered, "Go back to sleep; I've an alarm set," and gathered me into his arms. I closed my eyes again and snuggled into his embrace as sleep overtook me again.

Too soon, the sound of buzzing filtered into my dreams. I tried to burrow into the warmth next to me but then startled when it shook. I leaned back to find that the warmth was Henry, and he was laughing at me.

"It's almost 4:30 pm. I'm sure you want to change and fix your hair before the dinner. Plus, I remember you saying that you wanted to dress Matthew and Cora too."

I groaned at his words and pushed myself upright. We had just over an hour until the engagement dinner.

"I overslept," I muttered, already moving.

The next stretch blurred into motion. Clothes laid out, shoes hunted down, hair brushed while Matthew tried to escape and Cora insisted on changing her outfit twice. Henry moved through it with me, grabbing what he could, keeping the twins distracted just long enough for me to finish one thing before the next fell apart.

"Extra dessert if you cooperate," I said, crouching in front of them.

That did it.

By the time we were ready, Henry was heading out to pick up his dad, brother, and sister-in-law, and I was buckling the twins into their seats, reminding myself to breathe.

The hall was already buzzing when we arrived.

Voices layered over each other, laughter spilling from one corner to the next, the long tables filled with food that smelled like home and something new all at once. My mom moved through the room as if she'd been preparing for this her whole life, while Miriam added dishes of her own, the two of them working side by side as if they'd always known each other.

Matthew and Cora stayed close at first, then slowly ventured out, showing off their outfits, accepting compliments like they'd practiced.

At some point, I caught Henry across the room. He was watching us, smiling in a way that made everything else fade for a second.

It wasn't perfect. Nothing ever is. But it was full and loud and warm, and for once, I didn't feel like I was trying to hold everything together on my own.

By the time it ended, I was running on nothing but exhaustion and something softer underneath it.

I got the twins home ahead of Henry, guiding them through brushing teeth and pajamas while they talked over each other about the night.

Once they were settled, I lingered in the doorway for a moment, watching them finally go still.

The house was quiet again.

I leaned against the frame, letting the day catch up to me, a small smile pulling at my lips.

I still wasn't sure how all of this had become mine.

But it had.

Chapter 12

Six days later, Henry and I met Vincent for lunch at the local brunch restaurant where we'd eaten with his parents. He had chosen where and when to meet. We decided to open the conversation with our engagement, but then let Vincent guide the rest of the discussion. We didn't want to make him feel railroaded.

"Thank you for agreeing to meet with us," I began as I took a deep breath. I wore a casual sweater with jeans, while Henry had on a similar outfit. We hoped that a laid-back look would help with our news.

"We wanted to let you know we are engaged." As I said this, Henry picked up my left hand and placed it on the table where Vincent could see my engagement ring.

Vincent snorted and looked away. "Tell me something I don't already know. The news has spread halfway across town after the dinner your mom hosted on Sunday."

I let go of Henry's hand and sat back in my seat, surprised. No one had mentioned to me they knew about my engagement to Henry. I'd been to work, the coffee shop, and the library in the last six days. Maybe people were waiting for me to mention it?

"Well, I've news for you too," Vincent shared. "I'm moving to Kentucky, so you don't have to worry about me."

"What? You're leaving Belding? And Michigan? What about Matthew and Cora?" I exclaimed.

Shrugging, Vincent looked away. "I got a job offer and can make better money down there.

I can also live with my aunt and uncle for free. Seems like Matthew and Cora have a stepfather now, so why do they need me around?"

Out of the corner of my eye, I saw Henry stare at my children's dad in shocked amazement. I knew Vincent didn't care for the twins like a father should, but would he really abandon them by moving states away? I saw rage boiling inside Henry. His hands clenched into fists at his sides, which he hid under the table. I placed a hand over one of his. This wasn't his fight, even though I knew he loved Matthew and Cora, apparently more than their own father did.

"When are you leaving?" I inquired softly.

Vincent replied, still not giving me the grace of looking at me directly. "Two weeks. I just gave my notice at work."

Leaning forward in the chair, I braced my forearms on the table and glared at my ex-husband. "When were you planning to tell Matthew and Cora?" I already knew the answer.

Henry placed his hand on my sleeve and leveled his own gaze at Vincent. "Tell us when you want to talk to the twins and we'll make sure we are available." It was clear he wouldn't let the man get out of his responsibility. I saw Henry push back his chair, so I did the same.

Henry told Vincent, "If you've nothing else to discuss, I think we're finished here. We'll pay the check."

Henry led me outside, the tension vibrating off me. He drew me to the edge of the sidewalk, folding me into his arms. How did he always know exactly what I needed? I laid my head on his shoulder and sighed. Obviously, this hadn't gone as expected.

Two days after lunch with Vincent, Henry and I sat in the waiting room for my first ultrasound. We still hadn't heard from Vincent about talking to Matthew and Cora, but I pushed it aside. That could wait.

Today was about this.

I'd scheduled the appointment as late as I could, slipping out of work just in time to make it. The office felt familiar the moment we walked in: the same chairs, the same quiet hum; nothing had changed.

Henry hadn't sat still since we arrived.

While I filled out the paperwork, I could feel his attention on me. When I glanced up, he was watching everything — the forms, the clipboard, the way the receptionist spoke, as if he was trying to take it all in at once.

I smiled to myself and went back to writing.

Soon my name was called, and we went back to the exam room. The nurse took my vital signs and went over the paperwork. Surprisingly, once the nurse left, we didn't have to wait long for the doctor. It was the same OB who had seen me through my pregnancy with the twins, so she was familiar with me. I introduced her to Henry, but Dr. Antery was more interested in me and my information, though she wasn't rude to him. The doctor asked how Matthew and Cora were as she took measurements and reviewed the chart.

As she finished up with the exam, the OB considered both of us. "As I believe Dr. Ferrere mentioned, we would like to do an ultrasound to rule out a twin pregnancy since you had one the first time. Women who had a spontaneous twin pregnancy have a higher chance of a second."

"Yes, she mentioned the ultrasound. We discussed it, and we are okay with doing it. I scheduled it already for today," I said as I glanced at Henry, who nodded his agreement.

The doctor stood. "I'll have the ultrasound tech come in right away and do that. I'll be back when she's done to review the results with you both." She headed for the door and disappeared through it.

Henry looked at me. "I feel like I'm invisible."

Laughing, I put a hand on his cheek. "You're not. Dr. Antery is just a very busy woman, and she isn't used to seeing me with someone. Remember that Vincent wasn't involved with the twins. She'll come around to you."

Breathing a sigh of relief, Henry sat back in the chair as there was a knock at the door.

It opened to reveal a woman who wheeled in a portable ultrasound machine. She explained the process, and then pushed up my top, squirted on some blue gel, and rolled the ultrasound wand around my belly.

The tech talked throughout the time she did the ultrasound. She explained to us that she was taking measurements and pictures. When she was done, she helped wipe the gel off my belly and said that she was going to share the results with the doctor, who would be back in shortly. She also said that there would be a photo in the folder at the front desk for us to take home.

Henry helped me sit back up on the table, and I watched as he pulled the chair he was sitting in closer to the exam table. I reached out to hold his hand. Unlike my first pregnancy, this first appointment was taking much longer. Of course, I hadn't known I was carrying twins until after my second appointment. That had been when the bloodwork had shown higher than typical hCG levels, which had caused the OB to order an ultrasound.

The doctor brought me out of my ruminations on the past by knocking and walking back in. She was smiling, but in a congratulatory way.

"Well, Evy, it seems you may be one of those women that ovulate two eggs at once." Before Evy could process what that even meant, the OB gushed. "Congratulations, you're carrying twins again!"

Both Henry's and my eyes widened in disbelief. Neither of us knew what to say.

Dr. Antery chuckled. "I'll let you process that bit of information. I'd like to see you back in four weeks for a nuchal screening and regular checkup. You can schedule that on your way out. Leave when you're ready."

The doctor left us alone with the news of our impending parenthood to another set of twins, which had still not sunk in.

Henry was the first to recover. He slid a hand over my stomach and then stared into my eyes. "Twins? We're having twins?"

An incredulous, almost psychotic laugh escaped me. "How can I have another set of twins?

They told me the first time that spontaneous twins were a 3% chance. I know they said there was a higher chance of having them again, but I really didn't think it would happen."

Henry leaned his forehead against mine and closed his eyes. I could feel his breath merge with mine. His touch made the almost-panic begin to fade away.

"I've been meaning to talk to you about us getting bigger vehicles. Neither of our cars can really fit two toddler car seats plus an infant seat. Now we really need to get something bigger. I was thinking about a minivan or SUV," Henry leaned away as he said this.

"More like a van or minibus!" I exclaimed on a hiccup.

The two of us laughed at this, and it broke the shock of the doctor's announcement. Henry helped me off the exam table, and we left the room to schedule the next appointments before heading home, both thinking of the next steps now that we had this additional news.

HENRY

The folder they handed us on the way out didn't leave my side. I must have opened it a dozen times, just to look at the image again. Two small shapes, labeled A and B. Ours.

By the next morning, I was in full super-dad mode.

The kitchen table disappeared under it. Print-outs, notes, half-finished lists. Twin pregnancies. Car options. Floor plans. Anything I could find that might help me get ahead of what was coming.

I told myself I was just being prepared. It felt like more than that.

Every so often, I'd stop and open the folder again, letting my eyes settle on the photo before diving back into whatever I'd been reading.

Evy came home midweek and stopped in the doorway. I wasn't on the couch like usual. I was surrounded.

Her gaze moved over the table, the stacks of paper, the laptop, then back to me, her expression caught somewhere between confusion and amusement.

I looked up and smiled.

"Where are the munchkins?" I asked, getting out of the chair, walking over to her, and giving her a hug, laying my chin on the top of her head.

Hugging me back, Evy stood on her tiptoes to kiss me on the cheek. At the last second, I twisted my head, so it landed on my lips instead. I saw her glance at me before she replied, "They asked to play with Geneva, so Jonathan took them home with him. He'll bring them back in time for dinner."

"Wonderful! That gives us time to talk about everything."

"Everything? What are you talking about?" she asked.

"Remember when I mentioned cars to you at the last doctor's appointment? I've been researching them and have some I want you to look at. I also realized that we are going to need a bigger house. So, I went to the courthouse and found out who owned the surrounding property. I put in an offer and bought it all." I spewed out all that I'd been doing for the last week.

Evy put up her hands in front of her to stop my flow of words. "Wait, stop. You did what? You bought all the land around my house?"

"Yes. That way we can build a new home," I explained. I'd been digging through papers on the table and turned to Evy at the change in the tone of her voice. She was glaring at me, and I hadn't expected this.

"Henry Starling. Did you ever think of talking to me about this before going ahead with it?" demanded Evy. She now stood with her hands on her hips and a fire in her eyes. "You asked me to marry you. That means we're partners; partners do things together."

At this tirade, my jaw dropped. I'd only seen this side of Evy when she had talked to Vincent about Matthew and Cora. To hear her talk to me like this was almost unbelievable. As her words sank in, though, I realized she was right. I'd railroaded her and done what I wanted without talking to her first. I'd made decisions about our life without discussing them with her. I realized I had a lot to learn about being in a committed relationship. I'd truly never been in one before Evy, and we certainly had jumped into ours quickly.

Taking her hand, I sat in the chair and tugged Evy onto my lap. "I'm so sorry, sweetheart. I truly wasn't trying to exclude you from any decision-making. In my head, I knew I had the time to figure this out and take care of the details. I also didn't want to bother you with it and cause you stress."

"But I want you to bother me with the details. This is OUR life. I want to be part of the decisions. While I may end up agreeing with whatever you decide, it's still something we should do as a couple." Sighing as she explained this,

Evy ran the fingers of one hand through my hair while the other cupped my jaw.

"Vincent made so many decisions without me because he felt I didn't matter. I don't want to be, no, can't be, excluded in another relationship. The twins and I have been on our own for so long that I have become independent. I've become set in my opinion about things. But I want to share those opinions with you and debate what we want to do," Evy explained.

"I need you to see me and hear me," she urged, "Share with me everything you've done this last week. Then let's decide things together."

I took her face in my hands and kissed her. I then regarded the table, showed her all the research, explained my plans, and asked for her input. By the time the twins came home for dinner, the two of us had picked out the new cars, decided on an architect, and chosen a builder ... together.

Evy

By the next weekend, I still hadn't heard from Vincent. When I called him to set up a time for him to talk to the twins about the fact that he was moving, he tried to say that he was too busy packing. Henry took the phone from me at that point, seeing that I was becoming frustrated, and headed up the scheduling for the meeting.

"We're free tomorrow after church. Why don't you join us for lunch or after lunch? I'm sure you can take a break from packing on a Sunday." Henry was direct yet insistent.

There was instant grumbling from Vincent because of the lack of options, and he was now talking to Henry, not me. After having his few arguments shot down, he finally agreed. "Fine, I'll meet you at the park at 1:30 pm tomorrow."

The next day before church, I told Matthew and Cora that they would meet their father at the park after lunch and that he had special news for them. I didn't want to make it sound like good or bad news. The twins were just happy to see their father.

As expected, Vincent showed up late. I'd been staring at my watch, trying to decide when to call him, as he came strolling up to where Henry and I were sitting on a bench. The twins were playing on the toddler play set.

"Why are you late? Do you know how long we've been waiting?" I questioned him.

Shrugging, Vincent shoved his hands into his pockets and muttered an apology.

Henry left to go get the children, and I figured he'd done that in order to keep his mouth shut.

Matthew and Cora ran over and hugged their father's legs. "Daddy," they both yelled.

A sad smile crossed Vincent's face so briefly that I thought I'd imagined it. I watched as he got down to the children's level and gave them both a hug.

"Momma say you special news," Cora said shyly.

Vincent glanced at me. I looked back at him, refusing to acknowledge him. This was his news, and I wouldn't do or say anything.

Neither Henry nor I had sat back down on the bench. Vincent led the twins over to it and sat down.

"She's right, I do." And with that intro, he jumped right into it. "Kids, I'm moving."

"Move? Where? New house?" asked Matthew.

Vincent answered his son. "Yes. In a new town. In fact, a new state."

"What is state?" Matthew didn't know what a state was. I turned away during the conversation and pressed against Henry. On the next question from Matthew, I buried myself even more against him.

"Well, um, a state is part of where you live. Like this is Michigan. And I am moving to Kentucky," Vincent did not realize how much of a mess he was making of the conversation and how confusing this was for the twins.

Now I could only imagine that Cora's lip was quivering when she asked her question, based on the tears I could hear in my little girl's voice. "Is far, far away?"

There was a catch in Vincent's voice that I hadn't expected when he replied. "Yes, kiddo, it is. I won't be able to see you much anymore. But I'll still come visit when I can."

When I turned around, Vincent was hugging both kids tightly, and there were tears in his eyes. Maybe he loved them more than he showed.

Henry and I took a short walk and gave the three alone time to finish their talk and spend some time together. When we returned, we all went to get some ice cream, even though the twins had had some with lunch.

While Cora and Matthew ate theirs and were distracted, the adults had a brief talk.

"Vincent, we want to tell you something before it becomes public." Evy started.

Vincent looked at them both curiously. "More public than an engagement? What are you pregnant?"

Henry shot me a quick look, but I elbowed him surreptitiously. "We will be sharing this news next weekend, but want to tell you since you're the twins' dad. Henry is, well, he's a public figure."

"Public figure? Like I'm supposed to know him?" scoffed Vincent.

Henry stepped into the conversation. "Just because you don't recognize me right now doesn't mean you don't really know me. I've looked differently than you would expect most of the time that you've seen me. Let me show you a picture of what I usually look like." He took out his phone and brought up a picture of himself, then showed it to Vincent.

When Vincent saw the photo of who he knew as Ace Starling, he almost spit out his ice cream. "You have to be freaking kidding me! There's no way you're Ace Starling!"

Henry reached up and tugged down the sunglasses so they were on the edge of his nose. He had worn the colored contacts that he wore when he was the Vigil Warden. With his hair grown out and the changed eye color, it was more obvious who he was now. Vincent's jaw dropped. Apparently, that was proof enough.

Chapter 13

Evy

As the day of the film premiere drew closer, I became more nervous about it. The plan was to fly out bright and early on the Friday morning of the premiere. It would give us plenty of time to go to the boutique. Henry had already reserved time at it and put a few gowns on hold. We would then have lunch, rest at his condo, and then get ready with a stylist there before attending the premiere.

I wasn't nervous about the premiere itself as much as the fact that Henry was going to introduce me to the world as his fiancé. Before we left, we told Jonathan about who Henry was. He was the only person outside my mother and aunt whom I cared to tell in person. The reveal went better than expected, probably because Jonathan was much more grounded than those two. He just accepted that Henry was the actor Ace Starling, but also himself.

The next morning, Henry and I dropped Matthew and Cora off at Mom and Eileen's house with lots of hugs and kisses. This would be the first time I would fly in the jet. I'd heard about it, of course, but not seen it. It was unlike anything I'd ever imagined. It had two plush couches, two sets of spacious seats that faced each other, a table with four seats around it, two large flat screen TVs, full size lavatory, separate sleeping cabin with a full size bed, along with a section for the crew where there was a bar and kitchen.

Henry helped settle then buckle me in on the couch, and he let me know it was a five and a half hour flight. Once we were at cruising altitude, he told me I could move to the bedroom and take a nap, encouraging me to rest during the flight. After takeoff, I took advantage of this and lay down.

Sooner than I expected, Henry was waking me up to let me know it was time to land. He used a private terminal at LAX so we were able to de-board quickly and find Henry's car in the parking area. He had had a service bring it from the garage at his condo and leave it at the terminal.

As we drove to the boutique, which was in the Beverly Glen area, about an hour's drive from LAX, Henry reviewed the timeline for the evening. The red carpet arrivals started at 5:30 pm, but he didn't plan for us to arrive until 6:30 pm. There would be schmoozing during the cocktail time before the screening after arrivals. Henry didn't plan to stay to watch the movie itself, so we would head back to the condo when the screening started.

Pulling up outside the boutique, Henry dropped me off and went to park the car. He encouraged me to go in first, and he'd soon follow. The facade was very unassuming, being placed in what looked like a strip mall. However, walking in it was immediately obvious that this was a high-end store. It wasn't crowded—just a few carefully spaced racks, each piece displayed as if it had been chosen with intention rather than volume. A woman was standing behind a counter that featured jewelry inside it. She stepped out to greet me.

"May I help you? We have a reservation for the store right now, but I can set up a time for you to come back." The woman told me in a polite but firm voice while she looked at my outfit of forest green leggings paired with a multicolored tunic top. I'd chosen it for its flexibility in the weather between Michigan and California, but also because it would be a casual outfit for flying.

I took another step into the boutique. "I'm the reservation."

The salesperson raised her eyebrow and gave a slight laugh at this. "Pardon me, ma'am, but the reservation is under a man's name, so I don't think that's true."

I didn't move. "Yes. And he booked it for me."

Henry stepped in behind me. "She's right. The reservation's under my name—Henry Starling—but it's for Evy."

I looked over my shoulder, surprised to see that he'd parked and entered the store so quickly.

The salesperson frowned slightly, already reaching for her tablet. "I see. The reservation is under Mr. Starling's name, and no secondary name was listed."

She tapped the screen, then inclined her head. "That's my oversight. Welcome, Ms. Evy. Your fitting is ready."

"I asked for dresses to be set aside. Did someone really think they were for me? Go get the owner, please," Henry asked with a raised brow as he crossed his arms.

"Right away!" said the salesperson as she scurried away upstairs.

Within a minute, a tall woman came down the stairs to join Henry and me. She shook hands with us. "I apologize for my assistant. She is a very literal, black and white person. I'll talk to her later. She is berating herself right now and probably doing an outstanding job at it."

This made me chuckle, and I clapped a hand over my mouth, appalled that I'd let it slip out.

My guffaw made Henry laugh out loud. "Let me introduce you to my fiancé, Evy. Evy, this is the owner of the boutique, Joanne Parot."

"Fiancé? Well, congratulations to both of you! It's wonderful to meet you. I can see why Mr. Starling chose the style and color of dresses for you to try on. Let me go get them for you."

I spent the next hour trying on the five dresses the boutique had selected. It was quick to see that the one most liked by both of us was an emerald green gown covered in sequins that was sleeveless with a deep V-neckline. The waistband sat just above my navel, so the slight belly from the twin pregnancy didn't interfere with it.

The drive from the boutique was short, but I barely noticed it.

Henry parked in the garage, and we headed inside. The moment we stepped into his condo, I slowed down. It was... too much.

Open space, clean lines, everything intentional and expensive without trying to be. I turned slowly, taking it in; the scale of it pressing in on me in a way the jet hadn't.

This wasn't temporary. This was his life.

I knew he had money. Of course I did. But knowing and seeing were two different things.

At home, he fit so easily into my world. My kitchen. My routine. My life.

Here, I wasn't sure where I fit at all.

"What is it, sweetheart?"

I hadn't realized I'd stopped moving.

His arm slipped around me from behind, warm and familiar, grounding in a way the room wasn't. He drew me back against him, his chin brushing my shoulder.

I turned in his arms and took a breath. "How rich are you?"

His expression shifted, surprise flickering across his face before it settled into something more careful.

"Why are you asking that?" he said gently.

I shook my head, suddenly unsure. "I don't know. I just..." I glanced around again, then back at him. "I've never asked."

I started to step away, already regretting it. "It's not important. Forget I said anything."

"Evy, stop." His hand caught my wrist, not tightly, just enough to keep me there.

I looked down at where he held me, then back up at him. For a second, he studied me, as if he was trying to figure out what I really meant. Then his expression softened.

"I don't care if you know," he said quietly. "You never asked, so it never came up."

He reached up, brushing a piece of hair back from my face. "I'm worth about three hundred million."

The words didn't register right away. Then they did.

I took a step back before I could stop myself. "Three hundred million," I repeated, the number feeling unreal in my mouth.

Henry let his hands fall, watching me closely now. "That doesn't change anything," he said, more firmly this time. "Not about me. Not about us."

I didn't answer right away.

My eyes drifted around the room again, taking it in differently now. Not just as space, but as distance.

He stepped closer, slower this time. "You've seen how I live with you," he said. "That's not an act."

I looked back at him.

"I don't need any of this," he added quietly. "I just... have it."

Something in his voice settled that, more than anything else he could have said.

I let out a breath I hadn't realized I was holding.

"Okay," I said softly, though I wasn't sure yet what that meant.

He nodded once, like that was enough for now. "Come on," he murmured, reaching for my hand instead of pulling me. "Let's sit down for a bit."

This time, I went with him.

I had plenty of time to get nervous on the fifty-minute drive to the cinema where the premiere was being held. In just a short amount of time, I was going to be presented to the world, through the news and paparazzi, as Ace Starling's fiancé.

Was I crazy? I could handle being Henry Starling's fiancé, but Ace Starling's?

I definitely looked the part in the designer green dress. The stylist had arrived at 4:30 pm. I'd snacked while the man had shampooed, blow-dried, and styled my hair into a shining mane that fell down my shoulders like waves of setting sunlight. He had then applied makeup in such a way that it looked like I was hardly wearing any, but it still highlighted all of my features. I'd never seen such a thing!

Next to me, Henry was handsome in a navy blue suit, baby blue dress shirt, and blue satin bow tie. The lapels of the suit were also satin, which set it off as formal, along with the gold cufflinks that just peeked out when he lifted his arms.

As we neared the cinema, the traffic became more congested, and the car slowed to a crawl. We entered the line of cars for the red carpet queue and waited our turn. Henry told me the driver would stop, and he would then come around to open the door and help me out.

The driver pulled up to the curb, Henry exited, and then he opened my door. I stepped out into a thousand flashes of light as cameras went off. I put up my hand to shield my eyes from the glare as Henry looped my arm through his. Stumbling from the lights blinding me, I tried to right myself. Henry tightened his arm on mine and helped guide me.

As I needed to pick the skirt of my dress up slightly to ensure I didn't step on it, I straight-ened. Putting my other hand down to grasp the edge of the dress, I walked with him down the red-carpeted walkway.

I realized that all the people lining the edges of the carpet behind the gold posts were now looking and pointing at me. Adjusting my posture, I lifted my head. I WAS Ace Starling's fiancé and was proud of it. He had brought me here.

Out of the corner of my eye, I saw Henry smile at me and turned my head to smile back. We had reached the backdrop area where we would stop and pose for photographers. It was covered with the movie logo. Henry placed himself in the center of the backdrop and put his arm around my waist, drawing me close to his side. I could hear people calling out, "Ace, who's the woman?"

After the photographers took several photos, Henry faced me and pivoted me to face him. He put both hands on my waist, and I moved one to his chest as he leaned in to kiss me. Once he drew back, he studied the group of onlookers before stating, "This is my fiancé, Evy."

We ignored the shocked stares, exclamations, and questions that followed us as we moved off. We brushed past the press line, and I heard more questions being yelled our way. Henry disregarded them and kept walking with me at his side, holding my hand. He had done as he had promised and told the world about us.

Chapter 14

EVY

As soon as the jet landed, I took my phone off airplane mode, and it lit up like the Fourth of July.

"What the heck"? I exclaimed.

We had left LAX at 8 am Pacific time, arriving in Michigan at 4:30 pm Eastern time. While flying to the West Coast was an advantage, flying back east was a disadvantage with the time change.

Henry heard me and asked what was wrong.

Initially, I didn't respond as I was busy reading the text messages from my mom and Jonathan. Groaning, I looked at Henry with tears in my eyes. "It's the paparazzi. They're camped out at the house."

Hearing this, Henry growled, "I can't believe they found out where you live already! The vultures!" He tugged me into a hug. "Don't worry, sweetheart, I'll take care of this." Taking out his phone, Henry called Erik. He headed to the plane's bedroom and shut the door so I couldn't hear the conversation. I was too busy texting both my mother and my best friend to pay attention anyway.

How had this happened? Once we had walked past the press line and entered the cocktail area, Henry had introduced me to several people, only a few that I recognized and remembered now. The food had been wonderful, and I had had a great time, but all the attention given to me had been overwhelming. Being Ace Starling's fiancé gave me status no matter who I was.

There had been one awkward moment. At the cocktail table, a blonde-haired woman had approached us. She'd worn a form-fitting, strapless, shimmering gold sequined dress. I'd immediately recognized her as Rachael Westfield, the actress who had been in the first couple of Vigil Warden movies with Henry and who also co-chaired the charity with him.

"Ace, dear, it's wonderful to see you again. I didn't know you were attending this premiere." The simpering tone used by Rachael had grated on my ears.

Henry had slowly pivoted to face the actress. I understood he wasn't happy to speak with her, considering their history. "Evening, Rachael. It's great to see you here. The director asked me to stop by. May I introduce you to Evy?" He'd taken my hand and brought me forward so I was next to him.

When Rachael had reached out her hand to me, I'd shaken it. "Nice to meet you."

"So, I hear you're engaged. At least that's the buzz." The tone used then was less simpering and more questioning, almost a tone of disbelief.

"It's not just buzz; it's the truth. I just announced it." Henry had picked up my left hand and brought it to his mouth to kiss the back of it, showing off the engagement ring.

There had been a softening of the actress' face upon seeing and hearing this. Henry had been too busy looking at me to see it, but I had.

To both of our surprise, Rachael had then said, "Congratulations. At the gala, I was worried when you left so suddenly. Was it because you missed Evy so much? I'm glad that you have settled down. You've always been so serious, and it seems like you've found the right woman for you."

I had been the first to recover. "Thank you. Maybe the next time we're in New York City or Los Angeles at the same time, we can get together."

Henry had followed up with, "Definitely, we'll have to do that. You'll of course get an invitation to the wedding, though we haven't even decided when that'll be."

"Yes, of course, let me know as soon as you decide so I can put it on my calendar. Now, I'm off to talk to someone else I simply MUST talk to. Ciao!" Rachael had leaned forward to air-kiss us both before gliding away.

Unexpectedly, it seemed Rachael Westfield had been content to hear that Ace Starling was in love and happy.

As everyone had entered the theater for the screening, Henry and I had slipped out instead. During the drive back to the condo, I had closed my eyes. I'd felt Henry's hand close around mine, and he'd held it for the rest of the drive. The silence of the ride should've made me uncomfortable, but it had been comforting instead. At the condo, we'd both prepared for bed and immediately fallen asleep, despite the naps taken earlier in the day.

As we'd fallen asleep, neither had known of the plotting by the paparazzi to identify the mystery woman who'd accompanied the world-famous actor and how it would upset our lives. But now it was coming to light.

Henry returned to the main part of the cabin as the attendant let us know it was safe to disembark. He ran his hand through his hair and then rubbed his eyes. I watched him with trepidation, wondering what he had found out.

"Erik is going to call the local police department. He'll ask them to send officers to the house and have them set up a barricade at the front of the house for when we arrive. He's also going to hire some security right away. Evy, I'm sorry. I didn't think this was going to happen so soon. I'd hoped that it would take a few days or a week for them to identify you and figure out where we live. Then I would've had time to get things in place." Henry tugged me into his arms, tucking my head under his chin as he hugged me.

I felt better, though I was still nervous about what we would find upon arriving at the house. I texted my mom so there wouldn't be any surprise when the police arrived next door. She thanked me for the heads-up and let me know that so far the reporters had only paid attention to my place and not her house.

While the drive the night before had been quiet from contentment and fatigue, this drive was quiet because of stress and uncertainty. Henry turned onto the street to the house and immediately saw cars lining both sides leading up to it. There were also police cars in front of it with the lights on and people on the opposite side of the road. As we pulled up, it was apparent that Erik had told the police the make and model of Henry's car, as a uniformed officer waved the sedan over and then motioned for him to put the window down.

"May I see your IDs, please?" the officer said to both of us.

Henry and I handed them to the police officer through the open car window. The officer perused each and then gave both back.

"Thank you; we'll keep people back for you to enter the driveway and house, Mr. Starling and Ms. Braam. Please wait until we wave you forward." As she moved away, Henry put the window back up. It was, effectively, a shield between us and the world outside.

I felt slightly embarrassed by all the attention that was being given to us just to enter my home. I was also grateful too. There must be thirty or more reporters standing on the side of the road! How had they gotten there so quickly?

Once given the signal to drive forward, Henry pulled as far into the driveway and as close to the door as possible. "I'll get out first and go open the door. Once I get to the door and unlock it, run to it. It'll make it harder for them to photograph you, even with a telephoto lens. If you have a jacket, you can hide under it," said Henry.

I hadn't even been thinking about any of the paparazzi taking photos of me entering my house. I figured they would only be interested in Henry. Shivers and goosebumps made their way down my arms and spine while tears came to my eyes. *How did Henry deal with this all the time?*

Watching as he climbed from the car as he had described, I got ready to run as I'd been told. Remembering what Henry had said about a coat, I grabbed the cardigan I'd thrown in the back seat of the sedan and laid it over my head before I opened the door to run for the house. As I ran, I heard people yelling from across the street, but their words all blended together. I focused my gaze on Henry, and then, blissfully, everything became quiet again when he shut the door.

I took two steps into the house and crumpled to the floor before I began to cry. Henry took the cardigan from me and laid it over the nearest chair. Then he sank to the floor and held me, running a hand over my hair again and again until the crying ended. Helping me up, he led me to our bedroom, helped me change into pajamas, and tucked me into bed. I then heard him go back to the living room, shutting the door behind him.

Henry

In the living room, I called Erik before I could think twice.

If I didn't do something, I was going to go outside and drag one of those photographers off the street myself.

This was exactly what I'd been afraid of. Exactly why I hadn't wanted to bring Evy into my world like this. I should've known better than to take her to the premiere.

I paced the room, flashes from across the street cutting through the space, even through the glass. Swearing, I yanked the curtains shut just as Erik picked up.

"Henry? I take it things aren't good."

"What gave it away?" I snapped. "There are at least thirty of them out there. Evy broke down the second we got inside."

There was a pause, then the sound of papers shifting. "Security's already been contacted. Four guards by eight tonight."

"Not enough." I dragged a hand through my hair, already turning back across the room. "Double it. I want coverage at all times. And I want drivers. Bodyguards. For both of us."

"I'll make it happen."

"I also want the property secured," I continued, my voice tightening. "I don't want anyone getting near this house again."

"I'll start making calls."

"Do it fast," I said, quieter now.

"I will."

I stopped pacing and dropped onto the couch; the energy draining out of me all at once.

"Anything else?" Erik asked.

"No," I said after a beat. "Just... handle it."

"You got it."

The line went dead.

I let my hand fall; the phone slipping from my fingers and hitting the floor. I leaned back and closed my eyes.

Less than a day.

That's all it had taken to turn something perfect into this.

I pushed myself up and grabbed my phone from the floor.

I'd meant to go over everything with Evy. The cars, the changes, all of it. But that wasn't an option anymore.

We needed more space. More protection. Now.

I fired off a quick message to Erik with what I needed, keeping it short this time, then moved on before I could second-guess it.

At least one thing had gone right.

The house next door hadn't been connected to Evy. Not yet.

I called Maeve.

She answered on the second ring, her voice steady enough to ease something in my chest.

"The kids are fine," she said before I could ask. "They're asking for you both, but they're okay."

"Good," I murmured, closing my eyes briefly. "Keep them there tonight. We'll figure it out tomorrow."

We talked through a simple plan, nothing complicated, just enough to get through the next day.

When the call ended, I checked the time. Too late. I headed down the hall and paused in the doorway. Evy was still asleep. For a moment, I just stood there, watching her, the quiet in the room a sharp contrast to everything outside. I let her rest.

In the kitchen, I found something quick to heat, going through the motions without really thinking. It didn't take long before I was heading back.

I sat on the edge of the bed and brushed a strand of hair from her cheek. The touch was light, but enough. Her eyes fluttered open, unfocused at first, then settling on me. I saw the exact moment it all came back to her.

"Are you feeling better, sweetheart?" I asked.

Evy pushed herself upright, rubbing at her eyes. "I suppose it'd be too much to hope they're all gone."

"I wish they were," I said quietly, taking her hand and brushing a kiss to her temple. "They're not."

Her shoulders tensed slightly. "So what happens now?"

"I've already started putting things in place," I said.

She looked at me, one brow lifting. "What kind of things?"

"Security," I answered. "Tonight. Around the house."

Her expression shifted immediately. "Henry…"

"And when you leave," I added, more carefully now, "you won't be alone."

"A bodyguard?" she said, disbelief creeping into her voice. "A driver? Henry, I can't live like that. How am I supposed to go to work? To the store? To anything?"

"It's not forever," I said, leaning forward, trying to hold her gaze. "It's until this settles down."

She shook her head. "This is too much."

"I know it feels like it," I said, softer now. "But I've dealt with this before. I know what happens when you don't take it seriously."

Her arms were folded across her chest. "And I don't get a say in any of it?"

That hit.

I exhaled slowly. "You do," I said. "I just... I needed to act fast."

She didn't look convinced.

"I'm not trying to control your life," I added, quieter now. "I'm trying to protect it. You. The kids. All of you."

"Two SUVs are being delivered tomorrow," I said.

Evy blinked. "What?"

"We needed something bigger," I went on, too quickly. "With everything going on, it just made sense to handle it now."

Her expression shifted. "You already ordered them?"

"Yes, but—"

"Henry." She stared at me. "You did it again."

I exhaled, rubbing the back of my neck. "I know how it looks, but I didn't have time to wait. I was trying to fix things."

"We could've talked about it," she said, her voice tightening. "Even an hour later. I was in the next room."

"I was trying to take care of you," I said, softer now.

Her arms were still crossed over her chest. "That's the problem."

That stopped me.

"This isn't about cars," she continued. "Or colors. It's about you making decisions for both of us without me."

"I thought I was helping."

"I know you did," she said. "But it doesn't feel like help when I don't have a say."

I stepped closer, reaching for her. "You're right," I said quietly. "I messed up."

She didn't pull away, but she didn't lean in either.

"I'm sorry," I added. "I should've waited."

"You should have," she said, her tone softer but still firm. "We're supposed to be doing this together."

I nodded. "We are."

She studied me for a moment, then let out a small breath. "I'm not some fragile thing you need to manage, Henry."

A faint smile tugged at her lips. "Maybe when it comes to paparazzi, a little. But not like this."

That earned a quiet laugh from me.

"Let me be your knight," I said lightly, trying to ease the tension. "Just... with your permission next time."

Her expression softened, but she held my gaze. "Good. Because this is your second offense."

I winced. "Noted."

"One more," she said, tapping my chest, "and you're in serious trouble."

"I believe you."

A small smile broke through, and she leaned in just enough to brush a kiss against my cheek.

"Now," she said, pulling back, "tell me what you've set up. Everything. And we'll decide the rest together."

I nodded, reaching for the laptop. "Together."

Chapter 15

EVY

The next few days were busy. We had successfully gone to the church and returned home with the twins. The security guards had formed a wall, so the reporters hadn't seen us bring Matthew and Cora in. We knew the paparazzi had dug up information, including that I had two children, but Henry wanted to keep our pictures from the media.

A couple of hours later, the new SUVs arrived. They parked both behind the house, so the mass of people across the road couldn't see us as we looked over the vehicles. I marveled at the luxurious SUV that was now mine. It had a huge sunroof with a retractable shade, besides other features I didn't know how to use. The seats were soft leather, and it even had new car seats pre-installed. They were the ones I'd drooled over but never been able to afford. The craziest part was that I had this gorgeous vehicle, and I wouldn't be driving it for a while. I had to let the security guard drive it for now.

Matthew and Cora enjoyed climbing around in both vehicles. They sat in the car seats of both and claimed which was theirs. Henry and I laughed at their antics.

News of the reporters had spread through town over the weekend, so upon my arrival to work in a new vehicle with my secret squad (as I'd started to call the two women), there was less surprise than I'd expected. I was glad that I had women instead of men as my security detail. It would make it easier for me to have to spend so much time with them.

Gladys and Maria stayed out of the way but were diligent. They made eye contact with me when people came in to make sure they weren't anyone who shouldn't be there. I'd also been worried that the secret squad would interfere with my parent drop-off and pick-up. So far, the two women had stayed to the side.

Four days later, I woke up to find that I'd "popped." I tried to get dressed for work and discovered that my pants didn't fit. Any that had zippers, buttons, or snaps wouldn't close. Sighing, I dug through my closet until I found the only pair of pants that had an elastic waist. It wasn't the normal casual business-style clothes I wore to work, but it would have to do for the day. I paired the pants with a slightly oversized top that I hoped hid my belly and headed to the bathroom to finish getting ready before going to the kitchen to eat.

Henry was already making breakfast for Matthew and Cora, who were sitting at the table in their booster seats. He hugged me around the waist as I made myself a cup of coffee. I knew the minute he spotted the change in my waist. He palmed the bump that was our children.

"Hmm...what's this?" He questioned as he kissed my jaw.

With a groan, I twisted within the circle of his arms. I whispered since little ears were listening. "This pair of pants was the only one that fit! I wasn't ready for this to happen so soon. We haven't even told anyone yet."

Henry placed his forehead against mine. "How far along are you again? I should know, but I don't want to get it wrong and have you yell at me."

"Ten weeks. It's still almost too soon to tell people. They say to wait until after twelve weeks." I explained to him.

"At Halloween, it'll be over eleven weeks, right? Why don't we tell our family and Jonathan then? It's close enough to twelve weeks, and we'll only be letting a select few know. I don't know who else we'd tell anyway. Erik already knows. Maybe we can make the announcement part of a costume?"

I laughed at this last piece. Then I saw his face. "Oh, my gosh. You're serious? No way!"

"Yes, and no. Let's get one of those fun t-shirts and hide it under whatever you decide to wear," Henry suggested with a smile.

"That I can get behind."

HENRY

Halloween ended up being gray and cool, but not rainy or snowy. The twins had decided to be a princess and a pirate. I'd been the one to take Matthew and Cora out to get their costumes. When doing so, I'd discovered that the townspeople treated me no differently, despite knowing who I was. In fact, some businesses had put up signs that said, "Buyers only, No reporters" on the windows. My bodyguard kept the paparazzi from following me and the twins into the stores, and the businesspeople surprised me by making sure no one bothered me while shopping. If someone approached me, a store worker intercepted the person instead. At the coffee shop I frequented, the owner came out and told us to let her know if there were any problems. I told her to please treat me just like anyone, then she said that I was a regular and she just wanted to make sure that none of the riffraff in town bothered me. I realized I was truly a Belding person now and was proud to be part of the community.

At the house, I was surprised that it took so long to get Matthew and Cora ready for trick or treating. It took longer than getting them ready for church. Besides the costumes, the twins had to put on two layers of clothes under their costumes so they would be warm enough for the Michigan outdoors. Jonathan and Geneva also joined us for our trek around the neighborhood.

Outside, I stopped everyone for some photos before we took off. I found it telling that neither Cora nor Matthew asked me to send the pictures to Vincent. They asked me to send them to their grandparents, both Evy's mom and my parents.

As the group walked down the street to the first house, we passed the site of what would be our new home. Two days before, the construction crew had started clearing the area. The twins stopped and stared, asking questions about what was going on. Evy and I explained to them that a new, bigger house was being built for the whole family. Being young children, they accepted this easily and were quickly back to their search for candy.

I noticed a few reporters on the other side of the street following and attempting to photograph us. I sent one of the security guards to warn them off. Nothing would interfere with this family night.

Someone had warned me that the young children wouldn't trick or treat for too long. Just over an hour after we had started, we finished our excursion at Maeve and Eileen's house. Matthew, Cora, and Geneva ran up the stairs onto the porch, yelling "Trick or Treat" at the top of their lungs. Maeve and Eileen opened the door, pretending not to know who the children were, dumping a handful of candy into each open bag. Once they had their treats, the kids took off their masks and showed how they had tricked the older ladies.

Evy and I asked if we could all come in to warm up. In truth, we wanted to have everyone together to tell them about the pregnancy. The plan was also to include my parents by doing a video chat with them.

Maeve switched off the porch light as she was almost out of candy anyway, while the group filed into the living room. The parents permitted the kids to dump their candy, and we inspected it before each child selected two pieces to eat that night. While they enjoyed the sweets, the adults sat down to talk.

I started the conversation. "Evy and I have something to share. But first, I need to include my parents in this." I stopped and quickly called my parents on the video chat app that we used. Previously, I had told them I would be in contact with the excuse of showing them the twins' Halloween costumes.

Once my parents were on the call, smiling, I winked at Evy. "So, which of us wants to tell them the news?"

"Why don't we both tell them?" She suggested.

Evy undid her coat and took it off. As she did so, it revealed that she was wearing a shirt that said, '2 BUNS IN THE OVEN' and, I said, at the same time, "Surprise, we're having twins!"

Chaos followed the announcement. So many questions and exclamations flew at us that we laughed and had to yell for quiet. We called on one person at a time to answer a question and talk, starting with my mom and then dad. By the time we got to Jonathan, he had very little to say besides congratulations.

Back at our house, we sat down with Matthew and Cora and explained to them that they were going to be a big sister and big brother. Despite taking the time, we still didn't feel that the twins understood everything when they went to bed.

Evy

Five days after Halloween and the pregnancy announcement had been the nuchal appointment, which had found no chromosomal abnormalities. Both of us had been relieved by that news. Right after that, I decided to plan a special meal and celebration for Henry's birthday without his knowledge. I wanted it to be a surprise, but it seemed that he knew everything. His birthday wasn't quite a week after the nuchal appointment, on a Sunday, so I had little time to plan.

Framing for the new house had begun the same day as the nuchal appointment, and we had heard sounds of hammering, sawing, and the like every day since. It started at 7 am and went until 7 pm. The framing would take about two months, and I wondered if I would go insane listening to the noise.

Each day after work since deciding to have the party, I stayed out for an extra hour doing the planning and buying. I invited my mom, aunt, Jonathan, and Geneva to come over right after church. We would have lunch, cake, and watch a movie that I'd heard Henry mention he really wanted to see.

I stopped by a local bakery to order a cake, which agreed to do it as a rush order, since I had to pick it up in only three days. Mom would pick it up on Saturday, then keep the cake overnight and bring it over to the house after church.

I picked up the custom-drawn art of Hillsboro from the post office that I'd had commissioned and flown in from his hometown then took it to a store to have it professionally wrapped and then stored it in the back of my SUV so Henry couldn't find it. I had even planned an extra-special birthday surprise that I'd give him in the evening when everyone else went home.

Henry didn't question the additional time before I came home, and I'd gotten the secret squad to keep their mouths shut. I had impressed myself by setting up the surprise party without his finding out. As far as I knew, he had no clue that there was anything planned.

Sunday arrived, and I found it hard to behave as if there was nothing going on. I wished Henry a happy birthday and gave him a kiss on the cheek before making breakfast. I let him take on the chore of dressing Matthew and Cora while I texted to make sure all the other plans were in place. Lunch was going to be baked chicken with roasted vegetables and potatoes, one of his favorite meals. Jonathan had taken that on, and he already had it in the slow cooker at his place. I had coerced one of the house security guards to decorate the house while we were at church. I let him know where I'd hidden the decorations so he could set them up.

After church, I distracted Henry so my mother and aunt could head out ahead of us. They wanted to be in the house to set up the cake, let Jonathan in, and prepare everything before we got home. It took us some time to collect the twins and load them into the car.

Upon entering the house, the others yelled 'surprise', shocking Henry and scaring the twins. He began laughing and helped calm Matthew and Cora before hugging me. He also gave me a kiss and thanked me, as well as everyone else, for his surprise party. I handed him his wrapped gift that I'd brought in from the SUV.

"Do I open this now?" He guessed.

"Open, open!" Yelled Matthew. I rolled my eyes at my son, who had no patience at all.

Henry kneeled to Matthew's level, holding out the gift and requested, "Why don't you help me, little man?"

My heart melted at his asking Matthew to help with the gift opening. I swore that every day I fell even more in love with him. I watched as Henry's face lit up at the watercolor of his hometown.

"It's a…watercolor of Hillsboro," he breathed as he uncovered what was inside the wrapping paper.

I shuffled my feet and twisted my fingers as I admitted, "I asked your mom for an artist's name in town and had the person make it for you."

"I love it!" Henry exclaimed as he placed it on the coffee table and swept me up in his arms. "I just have to figure out where to hang it."

He looked down at me with love, and then around everyone gathered in the living room.

"You can figure that out later. Right now, let's eat and then we're all going to watch that new movie you've been talking about." I told him.

"We're going to watch it? Here?"

I rolled my eyes at him, "I have been listening to the hints you had dropped about wanting to see it. It's available to stream now."

Henry dropped a kiss on my mouth. "Thank you, sweetheart, I can't wait!"

"Well, you'll be watching it with most of us, just maybe not the kids, as that's part of your birthday celebration." I shared.

Henry's mouth dropped open. He apparently couldn't believe that everyone would want to stay and see a movie with him. This quickly changed to a huge grin as he swept the room with a gaze that encompassed all with its sincere gratitude.

Quickly, we moved on to lunch and then the movie, though the twins and Geneva were allowed to watch their own shows on a tablet in the twins' room. It was actually a romantic comedy, not something that I had expected Henry to be interested in, featuring two prominent A-listers. Soon, the adults were roaring with laughter. I begged for the movie to be paused so I could take a bathroom break. I didn't want to embarrass myself by peeing my pants!

When I returned, we decided to take time for the cake since the children had come out of the bedroom. Henry couldn't believe we had also gotten a cake for him. He declared this to be the best birthday he'd had in a long time. I leaned in and whispered, "It's not over yet either." When Henry gave me a quizzical look, I winked at him. My flirty vow was more a show than I felt. I hoped I could follow through on the promise I was projecting.

I spent extra time in the bathroom after the others left for the evening and put the twins to bed. I'd never been to the adult and lingerie store in town before I'd gone the other day. Previously I'd been too shy, and I hadn't felt a desire to do so. But for Henry, I'd put on my big-girl panties and gone in. It had been an eye-opening experience. I'd never seen or imagined many of the items in there. Most of the lingerie had been too revealing for me to look at, let alone wear.

I'd found one, though, that I considered to be provocative yet not too racy. Now I just had to find the courage, since putting it on, to leave the bathroom in my robe and enter the bedroom.

There was a knock on the bathroom door, and I heard Henry. "Evy, are you okay?"

"I'll be out in a minute. Just finishing up." I told him.

I listened for him to turn away before I opened the door. Entering the bedroom, I closed the door before turning off the ceiling light, seeing that Henry had already switched on a bedside lamp. I walked to his side of the bed, faced him, but couldn't look at him as I dropped the robe to the floor.

Henry had been sitting up in bed, propped up by pillows while reading a book. He'd looked up when I'd come into the room and then stopped on his side of the bed. When I'd removed my robe, he'd swung his feet over the side and spun so he was looking at me. I saw his eyes widen when he saw my outfit and then felt his hands grasp my hips.

The royal blue stretch lace teddy both hid and left little to the imagination. Its spaghetti straps and scallop lace V-neckline barely covered my chest, which was already showing signs of being larger because of the pregnancy. High-cut sides and a thong back showed off quite a bit as well. The stretch lace showed off my baby bump.

Henry hauled me forward until I was between his spread legs. I felt him put a finger under my chin and lift my head until my eyes met his. He ogled my outfit in admiration.

"Is this the rest of my surprise?" He probed.

I mouthed, "Yes," unable to say the words. My flirtatiousness from earlier that afternoon had fled once I'd put on the bodysuit. I felt dull and wondered if Henry saw me as prudish. While I'd tried to be sultry, I'd obviously failed. I wanted to be sexually adventurous for him. I just didn't know how.

I felt Henry's hands glide from my hips up my back and then back down. I caught the sound of his groan and saw his eyes darken with desire. He tugged me even closer as he kissed me, opening my mouth for his tongue. I felt his hardness press into my softness and moaned as my own desire heightened.

Henry fell back onto the bed and took me with him, so I was on top. His hands moved to cup my butt and press me into his groin. I moved my hips against his, making us both breathless. I sat up, and Henry's head followed to take a nipple into his mouth through the lace of the teddy. The combination of his tongue and the textured material was close to heart-stopping on my sensitive skin.

After switching his attention to the other breast, Henry peeled away the bodysuit by drawing the straps and upper top portion down. He rolled over to position me next to him and protect my slightly rounded belly. I found this endearing, but it quickly took second place when he moved to taking the rest of the material off me with his teeth.

The moves this man made were ones I'd only thought I'd see in a movie and not experience. I gasped when his mouth grazed the swollen and delicate area between my legs. I watched as he took his time to use his lips, tongue, and teeth to bring me to climax. Seeing him do this ended up being too much, and my head fell back while I kept myself braced on my elbows.

With my breathing ragged and my lower lip bitten by my upper teeth, I brought myself onto my knees and pushed Henry onto his back. I was so far into my passion and need that I lost my inhibitions. He shed his pajama boxers as I drew off his t-shirt. I wanted to do for him what he had done for me. Leaning down, I took him deep into my mouth. I felt the bed move as he fell back and heard an exclamation from him as I continued. Soon, moans alternated with cries of pleasure before he pried me away. I peeked at him through my eyelashes.

"Woman, you'll be the death of me. A death I would gladly enjoy." He panted. I practically preened at this and smiled to myself.

With that, Henry yanked me to my knees and kissed his way from the small of my back to my nape. He tugged my bottom to his hips and asked, "Are you ready again?" At my nod, he plunged into me from behind. I ached from his deep penetration, but also was desperate for more. Leaning back, I met his thrusts with whimpers of wanting to attain that pinnacle that was just outside of my reach. I heard the same in his voice as he drove into me until we both yelled out upon gaining that peak together.

Once our heartbeats and breathing had slowed, we moved onto our sides. Henry was the first to clean up; then he helped me. He gathered me into his arms, and I heard his breath next to my ear. "Thank you for the best birthday ever."

Chapter 16

HENRY

The following weekend, Evy and I went on a trip to New York City. We'd discussed having a weekend to ourselves after the overnight trip to the premiere. If possible, we wanted to do something every month until she was six months along. The construction crew had finished the privacy wall, so we felt better about leaving the twins alone, even with the lingering reporters. On this trip, I wanted to show her my place in NYC, and I also had to meet up with my assistant, Erik. It had been weeks since I'd seen the man face to face. We also figured it would give us a chance to do some Christmas shopping.

We left soon after Evy got out of work on Friday evening. It was only a two-hour flight to get to LaGuardia Airport. Once again, we went through the private terminal. Erik picked us up at the private pickup gate and put our luggage in the car's trunk. Our first stop was a restaurant for dinner.

At the restaurant, Erik and I took care of our business quickly. We both ordered whisky on the rocks, while Evy had a unique and delightfully tasty mocktail.

Erik left after he'd finished his drink. Evy and I leisurely enjoyed our dinner before wandering around the area, looking through the shop windows. Some shops had already decorated their windows with a Christmas theme.

"I've only ever seen New York City on TV," said Evy. "Every year I watch the Macy's Thanksgiving Day parade and see the window displays shown. But, being here in person and seeing them in front of me..."

I squeezed her hand that was in mine as she trailed off. "I know. It's magical, huh?"

Her sigh of agreement came out in a visible puff of steam. "Yeah."

We continued walking down the sidewalk. Suddenly, Evy stopped and looked at me.

"That mocktail I had at the restaurant? I always thought mocktails needed or would be boring and tasteless. That was the first one that actually made me think it was a cocktail. It was amazing!" She gushed.

I laughed at her enthusiasm. She smacked me on the arm. "Stop laughing at me!"

"I'm only laughing because you stopped so suddenly I thought something was wrong, and instead you had to tell me about the drink you had." I continued to grin at her.

Evy's face turned from annoyed to sheepish. She put her arm back in mine and dragged me back to walking down the sidewalk. I managed to put a neutral look on my own face. Soon, though, I saw Evy was yawning, so I wheeled us around and headed back to the car. Erik had picked us up in the sedan I'd sent back to NYC, and I'd sent Erik home by taxi from the restaurant. We headed uptown to my penthouse in West Chelsea.

Evy slowed the moment we stepped inside.

I'd seen that look before at the condo in LA, that brief pause where she took everything in and didn't quite know what to do with it.

The space stretched out around us, open and polished, the city spilling in through tall windows that caught the last of the evening light. The river glinted in the distance, and the High Line cut through the view below.

"This is… it?" she asked softly.

"Yeah," I said, watching her more than the room.

She turned slowly, taking it in, her fingers brushing lightly along the back of a chair as if grounding herself.

I stepped closer, lowering my voice. "It's just a place, Evy."

She glanced back at me, not fully convinced, but she gave a small nod.

I made a mental note anyway. If this was going to be ours too, it had to feel like hers.

That could come later.

Because it was so late after our long dinner and walk, we put away our luggage and settled in for the night.

"The main bedroom is on the second floor. It has an en-suite bathroom. I'll give you a tour of the rest of the penthouse tomorrow," I told Evy.

We had no immediate plans for the next day, so we didn't set an alarm and planned to sleep in, as there were no children to wake us. I knew the one thing Evy wanted and needed to do while in NYC was to buy maternity clothing.

The next morning, neither of us could believe we'd slept until close to 9 am. We felt rejuvenated and refreshed, then the shower we took together rejuvenated us in another way. I'd never appreciated the walk-in shower with a built-in seat in the penthouse main bathroom as much as I did that morning.

Over breakfast, I asked Evy what kinds of gifts she wanted to shop for while in NYC.

"I made a list of what I wanted to look for while here," said Evy, taking it out of her purse. "I'm hoping to get most of my major Christmas shopping done. Is that okay? Will it be a problem bringing it all back?"

Shaking my head, I took a drink of coffee to hide my smile.

She read off from her list: new kitchenware for her mom, a couple of books for Aunt Eileen, a tablet for Geneva, an e-reader for Jonathan, and toys plus books for Matthew and Cora.

I took out my phone and brought up a list of stores on my map app.

"There's a mall that should have stores where you can get all that, plus it also has a maternity clothing store. It also has a food court and a few sit-down restaurants for when we want to eat lunch," I told Evy.

Evy put the list back in her purse. "Great! One place to get it all done works for me."

I'd already made dinner plans for us. "I made reservations for us to have dinner at the restaurant Claud in the private dining room. It's not until six, so we have plenty of time to get our shopping done. If you're done eating, let's get going."

We were able to get everything that Evy wanted, and I was also able to help get the gifts for the twins plus a couple of my own for them. While she was doing her shopping for Maeve, I'd even snuck away to pick out my Christmas gift for Evy. I'd worn a winter hat while we were out. This was my usual while in NYC, and Evy had been skeptical about this since my hair had grown out. Usually, no one bothered me. However, today was different.

After lunch, we went shopping for maternity clothes, and I took off my hat since we planned to be there for a while. Evy was in a fitting room trying on outfits while I waited on a couch. Suddenly, a shadow fell across me.

I looked up to find a man standing a little too close, phone already in hand.

"Yeah," the man said, almost triumphantly. "I knew it. That's you."

My jaw tightened slightly. "You've got the wrong person."

"Don't do that," the man scoffed, stepping even closer. "I've seen you online. You think a hat's gonna hide you?"

I stood slowly, putting a bit more space between us. "I'm just here shopping."

"Right," the man said, lifting his phone. "So you won't mind a picture then."

"No," I said firmly. "I will mind."

The man laughed as if that were a joke. "Come on, don't be like that. It's just a photo."

"I said no."

The tone shift was subtle, but sharp enough that a couple of nearby shoppers glanced over.

Instead of backing off, the man's expression hardened. "Wow. Thought you'd be a little more grateful. People like me are why you..."

The fitting room curtain snapped open.

"Henry?"

Evy stepped out, her voice cutting through the tension. She took in the scene in a second: the man, the phone, the way I was standing.

Her expression shifted immediately. "What's going on?" she asked, moving to my side.

"Nothing," I said, not taking my eyes off the man. "We're done here."

The man's gaze flicked to Evy, assessing, curious. "Didn't know you had company," he muttered, then lifted his phone again slightly. "This'll get even more attention…"

"Stop," Evy's voice was sharp enough to slice.

The man blinked, clearly not expecting that.

"You heard him," she continued, stepping half in front of me without thinking. "He said no."

"It's a public place," the man shot back. "I can take a picture if I want."

"And he can tell you not to," she returned, her tone steady but firm. "So, how about you respect that and walk away."

For a moment, it looked like he might argue again. Then he scoffed under his breath. "Whatever," he muttered, lowering his phone. "Not worth it."

He turned and walked off, though not without shaking his head like he'd been wronged.

Silence settled around us again.

Evy let out a breath and turned to me. "Are you okay?"

"I'm fine," I said automatically.

She frowned, searching my face. "Henry."

I exhaled, some of the tension leaving my shoulders. "I'm fine," I repeated, quieter this time. "Just… annoyed."

Her gaze softened, but the concern didn't fade. "Does that happen a lot?"

"More than I'd like," I admitted.

Evy glanced in the direction the man had gone, her jaw tightening slightly. Then she looked back at me. "Maybe keep the hat on next time," she whispered.

A faint smile pulled at my mouth. "Yeah. That was the original plan."

She hesitated, then reached for my hand without making a big deal out of it, her fingers curling around mine. "Hey," she breathed, making sure I was looking at her. "We can leave if you want. We don't have to stay."

I looked down at our hands for a moment, then back up at her. "No," I said. "We're okay."

"You sure?"

"Yeah." My thumb brushed lightly over her knuckles. "Besides... you still need my opinion on that dress."

That earned a small smile from her. "Yeah," she said. "I do." But she didn't let go of my hand when she turned back toward the fitting room.

We quickly finished up the rest of the clothes shopping, then lugged our bags out to the car and back to the penthouse. Both the car and the apartment wrapped us in a sense of safety and security we needed after the altercation at the store.

That evening, dinner at Claud was marvelous. The private dining room was intimate, with a table that would only fit eight, but set for just two. It enclosed and separated us from the rest of the restaurant, ensuring privacy. The private dining room felt almost too quiet when we were seated, the door closing softly behind us.

Evy glanced around, taking in the small table set just for two. "This is... really private."

I smiled as I pulled out her chair. "I thought you might like that."

"I do," she admitted, smoothing her napkin over her lap.

A server appeared and handed us menus. Evy scanned it for a moment, her expression shifting slightly. "No mocktails?" she murmured, more to herself than to me.

I caught it immediately. "Excuse me," I said, looking up at the server. "Would the bartender be able to make a non-alcoholic drink? Something... creative?"

"Of course," the server replied without hesitation. "I'll let them know."

Evy looked at me, surprised. "You didn't have to do that."

"I wanted to," I said simply. "You should enjoy this, too."

Her lips curved into a small smile. "Thank you."

A few minutes later, the drink arrived, bright, elegant, and clearly crafted with care. Evy's eyes lit up the moment she saw it.

"Oh, wow," she breathed, lifting the glass. "This is beautiful."

"Try it," I urged.

She did, and her smile widened instantly. "Okay, that's amazing."

I leaned back slightly, watching her. "Good."

"So… what are we eating?" she asked, glancing around.

I hesitated only slightly. "I may have already handled that."

I had predetermined the menu for a chef's choice version when I'd made the reservation, aware that the prices may be a concern for Evy.

Claud wasn't a Michelin restaurant, but most entrees cost between $50 and $80.

Her brows lifted. "Handled it how?"

"I asked for the chef's choice menu when I made the reservation," I said. "And I made sure it was pregnancy-friendly."

Evy blinked. "You did all that ahead of time?"

"I figured you might worry about the cost," he added gently. "This way, you don't have to."

She studied me for a moment, clearly caught off guard. "I wasn't expecting you to think of all that."

I shrugged, though my gaze remained on her. "I pay attention."

Her fingers traced the edge of her glass as a small, thoughtful smile returned. "Yeah," she said quietly. "You do."

Our food had just been set down when Evy glanced up at me again, her fork pausing halfway to her plate.

"So…" she said lightly, though there was hesitation beneath it, "that guy earlier didn't seem like he was going to back off."

"He usually would've," I said. "Most people just want to confirm and move on."

Her brow furrowed. "Well, he didn't."

"No," I agreed quietly.

She studied me for a moment. "You didn't seem surprised."

"I wasn't," I said, trying to change the subject.

Evy set her fork down completely now. "Henry."

I looked up.

"You don't have to brush it off," she said gently. "That wasn't nothing."

A small exhale left me, my shoulders easing just a fraction. "It's easier if I treat it like nothing."

"That doesn't make it nothing," she replied.

I held her gaze for a second, then gave a faint, conceding smile. "Fair."

There was a brief pause before Evy spoke again, quieter this time. "What happens when... it's not just you?"

My forehead knitted slightly. "What do you mean?"

She hesitated, then said it anyway. "When it's the kids."

The words hung between us.

I leaned back slightly, my expression shifting, more thoughtful now. "You mean... if someone comes up like that, and they're with us?"

Evy nodded. "Yeah. Because that wasn't just annoying, Henry. That could've been scary... if a kid was there."

I exhaled slowly, considering that. "I try to avoid it when I can. That's part of keeping things low-key."

"But it won't always work," she said gently.

"No," I admitted. "It won't."

Evy's fingers traced lightly along the edge of her plate. "I just don't want them to feel... exposed.

Or confused. Or like they have to deal with strangers pushing into their space."

My gaze softened as I watched her. "They won't," I insisted. "Not if I can help it."

She looked up at me. "How?"

"We set boundaries," I said. "The same way I did today, just... quicker. Before it escalates."

"And if it does?" she pressed.

"Then we leave," I said simply. "No hesitation. They come first."

Something in her expression eased, but only slightly. "You'd really walk away like that?"

"Every time," I said without pause. "I don't care who it is or what they want. They don't get access to us just because they recognize me."

Evy held my gaze, searching for any hint of uncertainty. She didn't find it. "And what do we tell them?" she asked. "When they're old enough to notice?"

I thought for a moment. "The truth," I said. "That some people know who I am. That most are harmless. And that they never have to talk to anyone they don't want to."

Her lips pressed together briefly. "And if they get scared?"

"Then we make sure they know they're safe," I said. "With us. With family. With friends."

The simplicity of it landed.

Evy let out a small breath, some of the tension easing from her shoulders. "Okay."

My expression softened further. "Hey," I added gently, "we'll figure it out as we go. Together."

That pulled a faint smile from her. "Together," she echoed.

A quieter pause settled between us, deeper now, more grounded. And this time, when the moment softened, it held a little more weight, and a little more promise. They walked in comfortable silence for a while after leaving the restaurant; the night air was cool but pleasant.

"That was... really good," Evy said, glancing over at me. "Like, fantastic."

I smiled. "I'm glad you liked it."

"I did. A lot." She bumped her shoulder lightly against mine. "You might be setting the bar a little high."

"I'll take that risk."

A small park came into view just ahead, tucked between buildings, not far from the restaurant. I nodded toward it. "Want to sit for a bit?"

"Yeah," she said, already angling toward it.

We found a quiet bench beneath a tree, the faint glow of nearby streetlights casting soft shadows around us. Evy settled in, tucking one leg beneath her.

"So," she said after a moment, "Thanksgiving."

I leaned back, stretching an arm along the back of the bench. "Thanksgiving."

"Are we... hosting?" she asked, a hint of both curiosity and nerves in her voice.

"I was thinking about it," I said. "If you're up for it."

Evy let out a small breath. "I mean, I like the idea. I just don't know how we'd fit everyone."

"We'll make it work," I said easily. "We can re-arrange furniture, add a table or two."

She laughed. "You say that as if it's simple."

"It is," I replied. "Controlled chaos."

"Okay, but who is 'everyone'?" she pressed. "Because that matters."

I ticked it off on my fingers. "You, me... the twins, obviously."

"Obviously," she echoed with a smile.

"Your mom, Aunt Eileen," I continued. "And... I was thinking about flying my parents in."

Evy turned to look at me more fully. "Flying them in?"

"Yeah," I said. "I'll call them once we're back in Michigan. See if they want to come out."

She studied me for a moment, then nodded slowly. "Okay."

"Okay?" I repeated.

"Yeah," she said, a small smile forming. "Okay. We'll host Thanksgiving."

I grinned. "Now we just have to figure out the menu."

"Oh, that part I have opinions on," she said immediately.

"I can work with that."

"And we are not skipping dessert," she added.

"I wouldn't dare."

Evy leaned back against the bench, looking up at the sky for a moment before glancing back at me.

"This could actually be... really nice," she murmured.

My gaze remained on her. "Yeah," I said. "It could."

By the time the sun went down and the air cooled, we made our way back to the car and headed for the penthouse.

It was our last night in the city. We didn't rush it.

The next morning came later than it should have. We moved slowly, packing in pieces, neither of us in a hurry to end the quiet.

The flight home felt shorter than it should have.

By the time we pulled into the driveway, Maeve's car was already next door. I had just enough time to set our bags down before the front door burst open.

"Mommy! Henry!"

Footsteps pounded across the house, and then Matthew and Cora were climbing onto the bed, talking over each other before we could even answer.

We laughed, trying to keep up as they told us everything at once, their weekend spilling out in excited fragments.

I caught Evy's eye over their heads. The look we shared was quick, quiet, and full of everything we didn't say.

Chapter 17

EVY

A week after the NYC trip, we hosted Thanksgiving at our house. After dinner, we realized exactly how much we were looking forward to the bigger home. There had been seven adults and three children for the meal because Henry's parents had flown in for dinner after being invited. At best, the dining table fit six people, so Jonathan had sat at the smaller table with the kids. In another year, we'd be adding two high chairs to the mix. Plus, if Henry's brother and sister-in-law joined with their soon-to-be child, that was another high chair and two more adults for a total of nine adults, three children, and three babies. Way too many for our small home!

After dinner, we took out some board games and played charades. The latter became an escapade, and the board game was a recipe for disaster. Henry's parents chose to watch.

"Okay, no more sitting," I said, clapping my hands lightly. "We're doing something fun."

Matthew groaned dramatically from the floor. "Full."

"That's not an excuse," Henry said, nudging him with his foot. "You can be full and play."

Geneva popped up immediately. "Games!"

Cora bounced beside her. "Yes! Games!"

Jonathan laughed. "Alright, what are we playing?"

"Charades," I said, already reaching for the box.

"Rules," Henry said, holding up a finger. "No talking."

Matthew nodded seriously. "No talking."

"No sounds," I added.

Cora gasped. "No sounds?"

"None," Jonathan confirmed. "Just acting."

Geneva grinned. "Me first!" She looked at the picture on the card and froze.

"Oh no," I muttered.

"Go!" Matthew shouted.

Geneva started spinning in a circle, arms flailing wildly.

"A tornado!" Henry guessed.

She shook her head, then dropped to her hands and knees and started crawling.

"A dog?" Cora tried.

"No—wait—something crawling?" I said.

Geneva popped back up, flapped her arms, then hissed. Everyone paused.

"...flying snake?" Matthew guessed.

Geneva threw her hands up.

"Time!" Cora shouted.

Geneva collapsed onto the floor. "Dragon!"

"That was not a dragon!" Henry laughed.

"You looked like a dizzy chicken!" Jonathan added.

That did it; everyone burst into laughter, Mirian and John included from their place on the couch.

"Okay," I said, wiping my eyes. "That was… chaotic."

"I did good," Geneva insisted.

"You were something," Henry said.

"New game!" Cora demanded.

Jonathan reached for another box. "Alright, this one: Kids Against Humanity."

Matthew tilted his head. "Is it funny?"

"Very," Jonathan said. "But we're doing teams."

Cora immediately grabbed my hand. "Mommy and me!"

I smiled. "Deal."

"Matthew, you're with me," Henry said.

Matthew grinned. "We win."

"I've got Geneva," Jonathan added.

Geneva pumped her fist. "Yes!"

"Okay," Jonathan said, reading a card. "'At Thanksgiving dinner, don't bring up...'"

He looked around. "Adults, whisper the options."

Henry leaned close to Matthew. "Alright, your choices are... 'a stinky sock,' 'a dancing potato,' or 'someone's bad haircut.'"

Matthew immediately started giggling. "Dancing potato."

"Excellent," Henry whispered.

Across from them, I leaned toward Cora. "You can pick 'a glitter mess,' 'a loud burp,' or 'a chicken wearing sunglasses.'"

Cora's eyes went wide. "Chicken!"

I covered her mouth, already laughing. "That's a strong choice."

Jonathan crouched next to Geneva. "Okay, yours are 'a mystery smell,' 'a broken chair,' or 'a singing fork.'"

Geneva blinked. "A... singing fork?"

"Yep."

"That one."

"Alright," Jonathan said. "Let's hear them."

He pointed to Geneva first.

"A singing fork!"

A few laughs broke out.

Matthew went next, barely holding it together. "A dancing potato!"

Henry snorted. "Why is it dancing?!"

"My turn!" Cora shouted.

I leaned back, already laughing in anticipation.

Cora stood up proudly. "A chicken in sunglasses!"

There was a beat...and then chaos.

Jonathan doubled over. "Why is the chicken there?!"

"And why is it wearing sunglasses?!" Henry added, laughing.

Matthew fell on his back. "That's the best one!"

Geneva pointed. "Cora wins!"

I wiped the tears from my eyes. "Yeah, she absolutely wins."

Henry leaned back, still laughing, shaking his head. "I don't think anything is topping that."

The kids kept arguing over who was funnier, their voices overlapping, the room full of noise and laughter.

Henry glanced at me, watching me with Cora, smiling without even realizing it. His parents smiled at each other at the antics taking place in front of them.

"Okay," he said, clapping his hands once. "Next round. But I'm winning this one."

"No, you not!" Matthew shot back.

"Oh, we'll see," Henry said.

And just like that, the chaos started all over again.

Once it became late, Henry drove his parents to their hotel. They were staying for the long weekend and heading back to North Dakota on Sunday. The next day, Miriam had plans to spend the day with Maeve and Eileen before she and John had dinner out with the whole family. On Saturday, she and John would pick up the twins early and spend most of the day with them, giving Henry and me time to ourselves. Rather than doing anything together, we planned to wrap the Christmas gifts and hide them during that time.

Once the twins were gone, I faced Henry and brought up an idea I'd had and wondered about. "Henry, would you be willing to fly Vincent up after Christmas so he could spend some holiday time with the twins?"

Henry nodded. "Of course. If he wants, I'd do it in a heartbeat. For Matthew and Cora more than him."

"I'll text him and ask if he'd like to visit them. Once he replies, I can let you know what he has decided." Putting my hand on his cheek, I smiled. "Thank you."

Later, we cuddled on the couch and watched a movie, just enjoying the time alone. Suddenly, I sat up.

"Henry, I felt the babies move!" I announced with excitement.

Henry placed his hands on my stomach, though he knew he wouldn't be able to feel it. He had read in the pregnancy book that it would be weeks until he could feel movement. Leaning forward, he kissed my belly through my top and then tucked me once again against his side. We settled back to finish the movie.

When Henry's parents came back with Matthew and Cora, it was late, and we immediately washed them up and put them to bed. Both fell asleep right away. We called it a night as well.

The next morning, the twins didn't get up as early as they normally did. Henry snuggled with me, laying his head on my belly. He'd never looked so happy. His phone rang, and he rolled over to answer it. It was his parents, wondering when he would be over to pick them up for their flight home. He promised to be over in two hours, unwilling to give up this time with me right away.

The weeks after Thanksgiving settled into something quieter.

The house construction moved inside, the constant noise fading, leaving the days feeling almost normal again. I hadn't realized how much I'd missed that until it was back.

By the week before Christmas, there was only one thing I could focus on.

The ultrasound.

I left work early that day; my mind was already at the doctor's office before I even got in the car. Henry met me there, and for once, I arrived before him.

The paparazzi had mostly followed him lately, not me. My routine wasn't exactly exciting, and they'd learned that quickly.

But as I pulled into the lot and spotted a familiar cluster of cameras, I had a feeling today might be different.

I looked more like six months pregnant than eighteen weeks, since I was carrying twins. Because I'd been wearing sweaters and cardigans with the cold December weather, I'd hidden my bump. We both knew speculation and rumors would fly with us both at the health complex together.

Henry stepped out of the SUV first, scanning the area before turning back toward me.

"You good?" he asked, offering his hand.

I nodded, pulling my winter coat, which was tight on me, around myself as I stepped out. "Yeah. It's just cold."

His eyes flicked briefly to my coat. "That thing's not closing much longer."

I gave him a look. "Not helpful."

He smirked faintly. "I'm just stating facts."

I adjusted the front anyway, though it didn't do much. "I've been hiding it this whole time. Of course it chooses today to be obvious."

Henry glanced around again, quieter now. "We'll get inside quickly."

We started toward the entrance, and then the shouting began.

"Henry! Over here!"

"Is she pregnant?"

"Are you two expecting?"

"Is that why you're here today?"

My steps faltered for half a second.

Henry's hand tightened around mine immediately. "Keep walking."

"I am," I said under my breath, though my grip on him tightened in return.

"Henry, how far along is she?"

I let out a small breath. "They're not even trying to be subtle."

"They never do," Henry muttered.

A camera flashed too close, and I flinched slightly.

Henry stopped — just for a moment — and turned his head enough to be heard.

"That's enough," he said, his voice calm but sharp. "Back up."

"Just one answer, Henry!"

"Is this why you've been lying low?"

"Are you announcing today?"

I leaned a little closer to him as we kept moving. "They're going to figure it out."

"Maybe," he said. "But not from us. Not today."

Another flash went off.

"Evy!" someone called. "How far along are you?"

Henry's jaw tightened. "Ignore it."

My grip on his hand tightened again.

Henry felt it immediately. "Hey," he breathed, leaning closer to me. "Almost inside."

I nodded, keeping my eyes forward. "Okay."

"Are you hoping for a boy or a girl?"

"Henry, is this your first—"

The doors slid open, cutting off the noise as we stepped inside.

Silence.

I exhaled, the tension leaving my shoulders all at once. "Wow."

Henry glanced back briefly, then at the reception desk. "Are you alright?"

I nodded, though my hand hadn't let go of his yet. "Yeah. That was just... a lot."

"It won't always be like that," he said.

I gave him a look. "You don't sound convinced."

He hesitated. "It'll get easier to handle."

I let out a small breath. "They knew. Henry, they knew."

"They guessed," he corrected. "There's a difference."

I looked down at my coat, then back up at him. "Not a big one."

A small pause settled between us.

Then I softened slightly. "We're really doing this today."

Henry's expression shifted, the tension easing into something warmer. "Yeah. We are."

My lips curved just a little. "Are you nervous?"

He gave a quiet laugh. "A little."

"Me too."

He squeezed my hand gently. "Whatever it is, we'll figure it out."

I nodded, my thumb brushing lightly against his. "Together?"

"Always."

A nurse's voice called from down the hall. "Evy?" I glanced toward the sound, then back at Henry.

"Ready?" he asked.

I took a breath, then nodded, "Ready."

Inside, the basic exam didn't take long, and soon it was time for the ultrasound. The tech took the usual measurements, then asked if we wanted to find out the sex of the twins. Henry and I nodded animatedly, acknowledging that we did.

The woman eyed the machine and announced, "Congratulations. Baby A is a girl!" She then paused as she moved the ultrasound wand around my stomach. "And Baby B is also a girl!"

"Girls? Daughters! I'm having two daughters!" exclaimed Henry. Although my shirt was up and the ultrasound gel was still on my middle, Henry leaned over to give me a hug and a kiss.

I laughed at his excitement and returned the hug. "Yes, honey, girls generally mean that they are daughters."

The tech said, "Excuse me," and reached over to clean up the ultrasound gel and take care of what she needed to do. Henry leaned back to let her do her job. I hadn't realized until that moment that he had tears on his face. The emotion of finding out the gender of the twins had caused him to cry. It caused me to tear up as well. This man — the love of my life — continually surprised me.

We stepped out of the building into noise.

The guards moved first, creating space, guiding us forward as the shouting picked up again. Cameras flashed from every direction, sharper now, more aggressive than before.

Henry kept a hand at my back, steering me toward the SUV.

"Easy," he murmured. "Almost there."

I kept my head down and followed his lead.

The door shut behind us, cutting off the chaos in an instant.

For a second, neither of us spoke.

Then Henry exhaled and glanced at me. "We're going to have to address this."

I frowned slightly. "Address what?"

He pulled out his phone and turned the screen toward me.

A photo of us stepping out of the car was already online. Someone had circled my stomach, a bold question mark hovering over it.

My stomach dropped.

"They're guessing," he said. "But it won't take long."

I looked back at the image, then up at him. "So, what do we do?"

Henry's jaw tightened slightly. "We get ahead of it."

Henry texted Erik and asked him to set up a press conference for the next day. We would stream it live from my house. He asked Erik to fly in to assist with it.

Erik arrived early the next day. Mom took Matthew and Cora to school, and I arranged for the day off. At the rate I was going through personal days, I didn't know how I was going to handle maternity leave.

The living room had to be rearranged for the live press conference. Erik had set up his phone with a light ring and a tripod stand to help with lighting. He'd contacted major networks and feature providers who would connect to Henry's social media channels and stream the conference.

In preparation, Erik had written a script for Henry and met with both of us to run a mock conference. Henry would start, standing alone and reading the script. I wouldn't enter until he announced the pregnancy. Erik had purchased and brought along a maternity dress that set off my coloring and my baby belly in a sophisticated way. It was purple, which went well with my auburn hair, with a fold-over, off-the-shoulder neckline and bell sleeves in a light knit fabric.

We would share not only that we were expecting but also that we were having fraternal twin girls. The night before, we'd called Henry's parents to share the news and then gone over to Mom and Eileen's house to do the same. After returning, we'd called Jonathan and had also told him.

When it was time for the livestream, Mom came over to support me. Henry saw me standing to the side, wringing my hands while he waited for the signal from Erik to begin.

"Hello, I, Ace Starling, am doing this live-streamed press conference to address rumors that were started yesterday." He cleared his throat, glanced at the notecards in his hand with the script, then continued.

"At a film premiere in mid-October, I introduced the public to my fiancé, Evy. Since returning to her home, reporters and paparazzi have followed us for the past two months. Yesterday, reporters and paparazzi followed and photographed her and me outside a medical complex. Immediately after, a media site posted one of these photos, speculating about the reason for the visit."

Pausing again, Henry took a moment for a breath. He hated sharing details of his personal life, but knew that this had to be done before gossip ran out of control.

"Evy and I want to announce that we are expecting." He shifted his gaze to where I waited and reached out his hand for me to join him. I took a steadying breath, advanced forward to grasp his hand, and stepped to his side.

Tucking the notecards into his pants pocket, Henry placed his free hand on my pregnant stomach. Facing the camera again, he shared with all those watching the conference, "Due in May, we are having fraternal twin girls. We hope everyone can respect our wishes for privacy, especially during such a special time. Happy holidays to all, and thank you."

As soon as Erik let us know the stream was disconnected, there was an enormous sigh of relief from every person in the room. I excused myself to change out of the dress and into something more comfortable. Henry conferred with Erik about the next steps, which included addressing any news outlets that reached out following the press conference. When I returned, Henry let me know he was taking Erik to the jet so he could go back to New York. I gave him a kiss goodbye and told him I would take a nap after the emotionally draining afternoon.

Chapter 18

EVY

Matthew and Cora couldn't contain their excitement about going on an airplane. This was their first flight, and instead of being scared, they felt the exact opposite.

"Go above clouds?" Matthew asked.

"Yes," Henry said.

Both kids stopped walking.

"Above clouds?" Cora repeated, as if she wasn't sure she heard right.

"Yep."

Matthew looked at me, stunned. "Higher than birds?"

"Much higher," I said.

Cora's mouth dropped open. "In the sky."

Henry grinned. "Pretty much."

Matthew started walking again, faster now. "Best day ever."

"You haven't even gotten on the plane yet," I said.

"Uh huh," he said, beaming. "Best."

Cora skipped beside us. "See snow?"

Henry raised a brow. "Snow?"

"Like clouds," she said. "But close."

I smiled. "You'll see clouds really close. They might look like snow."

Cora gasped again. "Touch one?"

Henry laughed. "Through the window?"

She paused. "No touch. Will look."

They reached the gate, and the large windows revealed the plane waiting outside. Both kids froze.

"That plane?" Matthew whispered.

"No," Cora said, eyes wide.

Henry nodded. "That's your plane."

Cora grabbed my arm. "Go on?"

"Yes," I said, laughing softly.

Matthew shook his head in disbelief. "Me fly."

Henry looked down at them, then at me, a small smile forming. "Yeah," he said. "We really are."

Cora bounced again. "Go now?"

"Soon," Evy said.

Matthew grinned. "Me not scared."

"Me not too," Cora added.

Henry chuckled.

The trip to New York came fast after everything that had happened.

It was meant to be a break.

The flight was short, but keeping up with Matthew and Cora made it feel longer. By the time we landed, we were already laughing at how much effort it took just to keep them in their seats.

At the penthouse, the first thing the twins did was run to their room.

Henry had already had it set up for them. Two small beds, toys waiting, everything their size. They explored it like it was its own little world, their excitement filling the space.

"Mine?" Matthew asked, climbing onto one of the beds.

"For now," Henry said with a smile.

The next morning started early, like all mornings with them.

We let the twins decide what we'd do first.

"Santaland!" came immediately, both of them talking over each other.
So that's where we went.

The rest of the trip blurred together in pieces. Cold air, crowded sidewalks, bright windows, the twins' hands tucked into ours as we moved through it all. By the time evening came each day, we were exhausted in the best way, falling into bed almost as soon as we got back.

Too soon, it was time to leave.

We lingered near the door, bags packed, the quiet of leaving settling around us. I adjusted my coat slightly, then glanced over at Henry. "Can I tell you something before we go?"

He looked up at me, curious. "Always."

I hesitated for just a second, then smiled softly. "My favorite part of this trip was the skating night."

Henry blinked, a little surprised. "Really?"

I nodded. "Yeah."

"You didn't even skate," he said, a faint grin pulling at his mouth.

"I know," I said, laughing lightly. "That wasn't the point."

He tilted his head. "Then what was?"

My gaze softened, my attention fully on him now. "Watching you."

That caught him off guard. "Watching me fall on the ice?" he joked.

I shook my head. "No. Watching you with them."

Henry's expression shifted, quieter now. "Matthew and Cora?"

"Yeah," I said. "They've been skating before, but they still needed those little skate aids."

He laughed. "Yeah, those things are a workout."

"You had one in each hand," I continued, my voice softening further. "Holding onto both of them, steadying them, making sure they didn't fall."

Henry shrugged slightly. "They were doing most of the work."

"They weren't," I said gently. "You were."

He went quiet.

I stepped a little closer. "You didn't rush them. You didn't get frustrated. You just... stayed with them. The whole time."

A small pause settled between us.

"That," I added, almost to myself, "was the sweetest thing I've ever seen."

Henry looked at me, really looked this time, something deeper settling in his expression. "It didn't feel like anything special," he said quietly.

"It was," I said immediately. "It really was."

He glanced down for a second, then back up at me. "They were having fun. That's all I cared about."

"I know," I said. "That's why it mattered."

Another quiet beat passed. Henry's voice softened. "You were just sitting there, freezing."

I smiled. "Worth it."

He let out a small breath, something almost like disbelief in it. "You're serious?"

"Completely," My hand brushed lightly against his arm. "I don't think you realize how... natural you are with them."

Henry stilled slightly at that. "Yeah?" he asked.

"Yeah," I said. "You just stepped in like it was nothing. Like you've always been there."

He held my gaze, something unspoken passing between us. "I want to be," he said quietly.

My expression softened even more. "I know."

A faint smile touched his lips. "Next time... you're skating too."

I laughed softly. "We'll see about that."

"I'll hold on to you," he said.

I raised an eyebrow. "With both hands?"

He smirked. "Obviously."

I shook my head, smiling, then glanced toward the door. "We should go," I said.

"Yeah," he agreed.

But neither of us moved right away.

I glanced at Henry, and he was already looking at me.

There was a quiet kind of understanding in that look, something warm and steady, like we both knew this wouldn't be the last time we did something like this.

Henry

We flew from New York to North Dakota just after lunch; the shift from city noise to open sky happening faster than it should have.

Evy was quieter than usual beside me, her excitement edged with nerves. This was different for her. A new place. A new kind of Christmas.

"It's going to be okay," I told her, brushing my thumb over her hand.

"I know," she said softly. "I'm just… not used to this."

"You will be," I said.

That seemed to help.

By the time we reached the farm, my parents were already waiting.

My mother pulled Evy into a hug before she'd even fully stepped inside, my father close behind, greeting the twins as if they'd been waiting all day just for them. Within minutes, the house felt full, voices overlapping, laughter bouncing from room to room.

Later that evening, they insisted on showing Evy everything. The house, the land, the people who stopped by once they heard we were in town. It felt like half of Hillsboro had come out to see her.

By the time we got back, the twins were fading fast.

My parents had one last request before bed: their version of Christmas Eve traditions, already planned and waiting. Evy smiled and agreed, watching as they carried it out with quiet excitement.

Once the twins were finally asleep, the house settled.

We sat together for a while, talking about everything and nothing. The pregnancy. Work. The way life had shifted so quickly for all of us.

It was later than any of us had intended when my parents finally led us upstairs.

Evy was already yawning as I helped her change, her movements slower, heavier with exhaustion. I eased her into bed, smoothing her hair back from her face.

"Thank you," she murmured.

I slid in beside her, and she curled into me without hesitation. Within minutes, she was asleep.

The next morning came too early as yells and screams accompanied two bodies hitting the mattress, waking us up. I rolled to protect Evy from the onslaught.

"Santa came!" yelled Matthew.

"Mommy, wake up! Henry!" followed up Cora, not to be outdone by her brother.

The two yanked on us, trying to remove us from the warm covers. They knew they wouldn't be able to open any presents without permission.

I brushed a chunk of hair away from my forehead and tried to pick up my phone from the bedside stand. "What time is it?"

"It doesn't matter. It's Christmas morning," replied Evy. She rubbed the sleep from her eyes and looked over my arm to see the time as well. "Oh, my. 4:36 am?" She groaned and fell back against the pillow. It was worse than I had expected.

"Holy crap," I said under my breath as I ran a hand down my face.

"Welcome to fatherhood," muttered Evy.

Grabbing her own phone off the stand next to her side of the bed, Evy set an alarm for 7:30 am and gave it to her children. "It is too early to open any gifts. Granny and Grandad will sleep for a few more hours. Gramma and Aunt Eileen won't be here for five more hours. Go back to your room until this alarm goes off."

Pouts appeared on both of the tiny faces, but they knew better than to argue. Cora took her mom's phone, and the two walked dejectedly out of the room. Sliding back under the covers, I spooned Evy. She could feel my heartbeat and her own slowing down after the unexpected waking up, and we both drifted back to sleep.

Too soon the twins were back, holding the phone with the alarm going off. It was a much better awakening than the yelling that had happened before. Stretching, Evy took her phone back and then told the children to wait for us in the living room.

"Don't touch or open any gifts until we get there. Also, don't be too loud; your grandparents are still sleeping," she warned them. As they ran off, she sleepily looked at me. "Ready for your first Christmas morning chaos?"

Evy and I put on robes and headed to the living room. I stopped in the kitchen to start coffee and hot water for tea. Evy continued on to make sure the twins had followed her instructions. She found Miriam and John already there. They let Matthew and Cora find and sort the presents. Since they could identify their names, they allowed them to find theirs and put them in a pile. They would sort the rest later.

The adults sipped their beverages and laughed while the children divided the gifts. They took a while, but after they made the small stacks, each kid got to pick one to open until their gramma and great-aunt arrived. This appeased them and kept them occupied until Maeve and Eileen arrived an hour later.

The rest of the morning buzzed with wrapping paper, bows, and ribbons flying around, gifts on display, laughter, and conversation.

"Okay, this mine!" Matthew declared, diving across the floor toward a wrapped box.

"Hey!" Cora protested. "That mine!"

"Is not..." Matthew flipped it over, then froze. "...oh."

Cora giggled. "Alright, alright," I laughed, stepping in before it escalated. "Name-reading is step one, buddy."

Wrapping paper flew as ribbons were torn loose and bows popped off. "I got it!" Cora cheered, holding up a stuffed animal. "Look!"

"That's adorable," Evy said warmly.

Matthew finally tore into his present. "Whoa, cool!"

The room buzzed with noise, laughter, overlapping voices, and paper crinkling underfoot.

I leaned back slightly, taking it all in before reaching for one of the gifts set aside for me.

Evy watched me carefully. "Open that one."

I tore the paper back, revealing a folded t-shirt. I blinked, then held it up. "'DAD4?'" I read aloud, a slow grin spreading across my face. I laughed under my breath, shaking my head. "Guess I don't get to ease into it."

Evy smiled. "Not even a little."

I set the shirt aside, still smiling, then reached for the next box. "This one too?" I asked.

Evy nodded, quieter now. "Yeah."

I opened it more carefully this time. Inside was a carved sculpture. I stilled. The room noise seemed to fade just a little as I lifted it out, turning it slightly in my hands. "A couple..." I said slowly, taking it in. "Twins... and..."

"Another set," Evy finished softly.

I looked up at her. "You had this made?"

She nodded. "As soon as we found out."

I glanced back down at it, my thumb brushing lightly over the carved figures. "This is... Evy."

"I wasn't sure it would make it in time," she admitted. "I kind of paid an unreasonable amount to rush it."

I huffed a quiet laugh, though my eyes hadn't left it. "Worth it."

A brief pause settled between us before I set the sculpture down carefully. "Alright," I said, reaching for another box. "Your turn."

She narrowed her eyes playfully. "This had better not be something that makes me cry in front of everyone."

"No promises," I said.

She laughed and opened it, peeling back the paper. Inside was a small velvet box. Her hands slowed. "Henry..." she murmured.

"Just open it," I insisted gently.

Inside, the necklace caught the light—white gold and rose gold, delicate and intentional. Evy stared at it for a moment. "This is..."

I leaned forward slightly. "I didn't want to do the typical birthstone thing."

She looked up at me. "The center circle is you," I said. "And the two smaller ones... for them."

Her fingers brushed lightly over the piece. "It's beautiful."

"They're connected," I added. "All of it. Just... made it feel right."

Evy swallowed slightly, her voice softer now. "You thought all that through?"

"Yeah," I said simply.

She closed the box gently for a second, then opened it again as if she needed to see it twice. "I love it," she said, meeting my eyes. "I really love it."

I smiled, something warm and steady in it. "Good."

"Will you help me put it on?" she asked.

"Of course." I stepped behind her as she lifted her hair, the noise of the room continuing around us, but softer now, like it had pulled back. As I fastened the clasp, my fingers brushed lightly against her neck. "There," I whispered.

Evy touched the necklace, her lips curving into a small smile. "It's perfect."

I stepped back, my gaze lingering on her for just a second longer. "Yeah," I said softly. "It is."

Across the room, Matthew shouted, "More presents!"

And just like that, the mayhem of the present opening rushed back in.

We had an early Christmas dinner before heading back.

No one lingered the way we had the night before. There was a quiet sense that things were winding down, that the holiday was already slipping away.

The flight home felt faster than it should have. By the time we landed, real life was already waiting.

Evy would be back at work in the morning, the daycare running as if nothing had changed. The brief moment we'd had was over.

Friday loomed next. That was when Vincent would arrive.

Matthew and Cora talked about it the entire ride home, their excitement spilling over as they counted down the days.

I listened, watching them in the rearview mirror. Evy reached for my hand. Neither of us said anything.

Evy

My birthday fell on a Thursday in early January. I hadn't taken the day off. After the holidays, it didn't feel right to ask for more time away, even if Henry clearly had other ideas.

He didn't say anything at first. He just told me to pack a bag. By that evening, we were on a plane to New York.

"This might be your last chance to get away before they get here," he said, glancing at my stomach with a small smile.

I rested my hand there, feeling the weight of it, a quiet reminder that everything was changing.

"I'm glad you didn't ask," I admitted softly.

The penthouse was quiet when we arrived. Dinner came in boxes, eaten side by side on the couch, neither of us bothering with plates. It felt easy. Uncomplicated.

The next morning, I woke to the smell of coffee and something warm.

Henry appeared at the bedroom door with a tray, a little too pleased with himself.

"Breakfast in bed?" I teased.

"Don't get used to it," he said, setting it down anyway.

I smiled and shifted against the pillows, more tired than I wanted to admit. Everything felt heavier lately. Slower.

Later, I found racks of clothes lining one wall of the living room.

I stopped short. "Henry…"

He glanced up from where he was sitting. "Before you say anything, I wasn't dragging you through stores."

I ran my hand over one of the hangers, half-laughing. "You brought the stores to me?"

"Seemed easier."

It was.

I sank into the couch and started sorting through everything, grateful in a way I didn't quite have the words for.

The rest of the day passed quietly.

Movies. Takeout. His hands working the tension out of my feet while I half-dozed against the cushions. Later, warm water and quiet laughter in the oversized tub, the world outside felt very far away.

It wasn't the kind of birthday I would have planned.

It was better. By the time we flew home, I felt lighter somehow. Like I could breathe again.

Chapter 19

HENRY

Over the next six weeks, we grew even closer as a couple. Evy had doctor check-ups with ultrasounds every three weeks, which I went to. The girls' development and growth were going well. We also met with the interior designer to pick out flooring, tile, trim, siding, shingles, and other materials for the house. She would share our choices with the builder.

However, in the second week of February, reality interrupted our peace when my agent called to inform me that filming would begin in two and a half weeks. We'd known that this would come, but had lost track of time.

I stared at my phone for a second after the call ended.

Evy noticed immediately. "That didn't sound like a casual check-in."

I exhaled slowly. "It wasn't."

She set her book down. "What happened?"

"They're starting filming," I said. "In two and a half weeks."

Evy blinked. "That soon?"

"Yeah."

A small silence settled between us. "We knew it was coming," she said.

"I know," I replied. "I just... didn't think it would feel like this."

She shifted closer to me on the couch. "Like what?"

"Like I'm about to miss everything," I admitted.

Evy's expression softened. "Henry..."

"I already convinced them to let me start later," I continued. "I'm leaving the day after your next appointment."

Her eyebrows lifted slightly. "You moved your start date?"

"A little," I said. "I wasn't missing that one."

Her lips curved faintly. "You didn't have to do that."

"Yeah," I said, meeting her eyes, "I did."

She held my gaze for a moment, something warm but heavy passing between us. "Thank you."

I nodded once, then leaned back, running a hand through my hair. "It's still not enough."

Evy frowned. "What do you mean?"

"I'm going to miss others," I said. "More than a couple, probably."

"How long?" she asked instead. She didn't need to finish the whole question.

"Fifty days," I said. "A little over seven weeks."

Her breath caught slightly. "Seven weeks…"

"Yeah," Another pause. I looked down at my hands. "I'm going to try to come back once or twice. Weekends, if they'll let me."

"But you don't know if they will," she said quietly.

"No," I admitted.

Evy leaned back against the couch, processing. "That's… a long time."

"It is." The room felt quieter now. I let out a frustrated breath. "A week sounds long to me right now."

Evy gave a small, understanding smile. "I was just thinking that."

I glanced at her. "You're not… upset?"

"With you?" she asked.

"Yeah."

She shook her head. "No. This is your job, Henry. It's not like you chose the timing."

"Still feels like I did," I muttered.

Evy reached for my hand, lacing her fingers with mine. "You didn't."

I squeezed her hand, but my jaw remained tight. "I don't want to miss things."

"You won't miss everything," she said gently.

"I'll miss enough," I replied.

Her thumb brushed over my knuckles. "Then we'll make up for it."

I looked at her, searching. "How?"

"We call," she said. "We FaceTime. We keep you involved in everything, however we can."

I gave a faint huff. "That's not the same."

"No," she admitted. "It's not. But it's something."

I went quiet again.

Evy shifted a little closer. "And when you're here... you're here. No distractions. No half attention."

That pulled my gaze back to hers. "I already do that," I said.

"I know," she whispered. "That's why we'll be okay."

I studied her for a long moment, then nodded slowly. "Just..." I started, then stopped.

"What?" she asked.

I hesitated, then said it anyway. "I don't like the idea of being that far away from you right now."

Her expression softened completely at that. "Me neither," she admitted. A quiet beat passed. "But we'll get through it," she added.

I let out a slow breath, some of the tension easing. "Yeah," I said. "We will."

She squeezed my hand again. "And you're not missing the upcoming appointment."

"Not a chance."

"Good," she said, a small smile returning.

I leaned my head back against the couch, still holding her hand. "Seven weeks," I muttered.

Evy leaned lightly against my shoulder. "One day at a time."

I turned my head slightly toward her. "You're going to keep saying that, aren't you?"

"Probably," she said.

A faint smile finally broke through. "Alright," I said. "One day at a time."

With the deadline of leaving looming ahead, there were suddenly so many things to do. Checking the progress of the house, making sure the security company had everything in place, and talking to Jonathan about doing regular visits with Evy were just a few of the items on my list.

Too soon, the date of the next ultrasound and doctor's appointment arrived. It confirmed that everything continued to go fine, despite my fretting about Evy's swollen ankles and slightly elevated blood pressure. I seemed to want to find a reason for me not to have to leave.

That evening I picked up dinner, telling Matthew and Cora that they were having a special meal since I was leaving the next day. We ate it on the floor of the living room, picnic-style.

"Where going, Henry?" inquired Cora. As the quieter one, it was unusual for her to ask the first question.

Putting her on my lap, I tucked her under my chin. *I was going to miss this so much.* "Well, munchkin, I have to go to work for a while. For maybe a long while."

"What job?" Countered Matthew, never one to be left out.

"I'm an actor. Like on your TV shows, but I make movies."

At this, the twins' eyes went wide. They knew this was a big deal, but obviously they didn't understand exactly how big a deal I was as a movie star.

Gathering Matthew up as well, I hugged both children. "I'm going to miss both of you, plus your mommy SO much." Kissing their heads, I blinked at Evy with tears in my eyes.

That night, I lay with Evy's head on my chest. Her belly rested on my stomach, and then I felt a hit. Evy's head lifted, and her arm brought my hand to where the movement had come from. Smiling, she peered at me. "Did you feel that?"

My face showed the awe I felt. "Yeah." Lying back down, I kept my hand under hers, feeling a few more kicks, wondering if they were coming from one or both of my girls.

The next morning, I had to leave bright and early, almost an hour before Evy, Matthew, and Cora had to leave for the daycare building. Evy got up with me, but we let the twins sleep. It was a quiet breakfast as we held hands. When it was time for me to leave, I briefly woke the children for a hug and kiss before giving the same to Evy. I then tore myself away, trying not to look back as I drove to the airport.

I called and video chatted with Evy and the twins every day if I could. Evy informed me about her latest doctor's appointment two weeks after I left, as the appointments had increased to every other week, but she didn't need ultrasounds for each one. We chatted about everyday life, and I promised I'd be back for the twins' birthday in a week and a half.

The next day, I planned to talk to the director about taking a few days off to return home to spend time with my family. I caught him between takes, stepping in before he could disappear behind the monitors.

"Hey, do you have a minute?" I asked.

The director glanced at me, already distracted. "Make it quick."

"I need to talk about the schedule," I said. "I was hoping to take a couple of days — two, maybe three — to go home."

The director's expression didn't change. "That's not going to work."

My jaw tightened slightly. "It's important."

"It's always important," the director replied, flipping through a clipboard. "We're already tight. If you're gone for that long, we lose momentum."

"It's a few days," I pressed. "We can shift scenes."

"No," the director said flatly. "We can't."

A beat passed. I took a breath, trying again. "Then one or two days. I just need to get back…"

"You can take one," the director cut in. "One day. That's it."

I stared at him. "One day?"

"Yes."

"That's barely enough time to get there and back."

"Then make it count," the director said, already starting to move past me. "We're shooting every day. You knew that when you signed on."

I stepped slightly into his path. "I didn't know it would be like this."

The director paused, irritation flickering. "It's always like this."

Silence stretched between us. I nodded once, tightly. "Right."

"Good," the director said. "Then we're clear." He walked off without another word.

I stood there for a moment, unmoving. Then I turned sharply and walked down the corridor, past crew members, past closed doors, until I found an empty stretch of wall.

I stopped. For a second, I just stood there, breathing. Then...

Thud.

My fist slammed into the wall. Pain shot up my arm, but I barely reacted. "Damn it," I muttered under my breath. I leaned forward, resting my forehead briefly against the wall, eyes squeezed shut. "This was a mistake," I said quietly.

A crew member passing nearby hesitated. "You okay, man?"

I straightened immediately, masking it. "Yeah. I'm fine."

The guy nodded, unsure, then kept walking.

I flexed my hand once, wincing slightly. "Seven weeks," I muttered. "For this." I let out a sharp breath, frustration still simmering just beneath the surface. The words hung there, quiet but heavy.

After a moment, I pushed myself off the wall, rolling my shoulders as if I could shake it off. But the tension stayed with me as I headed back toward the set.

A week later, I was on my jet to fly home for only a few hours. I'd spend eleven hours of the day flying. It still annoyed me that the director had told me I couldn't stay longer. I knew we were on a deadline, but I didn't understand why they couldn't have rearranged the schedule so that they wouldn't need me for two or three days.

Once the jet landed, I was ready to drive as fast as I could back to my home. The forty-five minute drive seemed to take forever. When I pulled into the driveway, the door to the house flew open before I'd even put the SUV into park. Cora and Matthew were the first out the door and running to me. Evy was slightly behind them, taking her time because of her bulk.

In just the three and a half weeks I'd been gone, I could see that she had grown slightly larger. She was a bit more than the size of a full-term pregnancy at this point and still had nine weeks to go. I saw the glow that she'd gained from carrying my children, but also the tiredness that must be from handling these last few weeks herself. Her mom, aunt, and best friend were helping as much as they could, but she still had a lot that she was doing on her own.

I scooped up both children, one in each arm. I hugged them close to me, overwhelmed with emotion. Leaving my car door open, I continued walking towards the house, closer to the woman I loved. I met up with Evy and put the children down to draw her into an embrace. Our mouths met in a kiss. Her arms twined around my neck while my hands cupped her face.

I'd missed this — her — so much. The feel of her skin, the smell of her, the way her breath caught when I touched her. I knew we couldn't do much more than this, but it didn't matter. She was here, in my arms, where she belonged. It was going to break me when I had to leave in a few hours.

We finally ran out of breath and had to step apart. The twins were each holding onto one of my legs. I walked back to the car just like that, dragging them along. I'd brought no luggage, but had to shut the car door, not wishing to kill the battery. The birthday party was in a couple of hours, so we had some time to spend as a family.

Inside, Matthew and Cora showed me all the art they'd done at daycare since I'd been gone. Evy sat with me on the couch, smiling as she watched them share these with me. I felt more like a father to them than their own. I knew I loved them like that, too.

The three had gotten up early to get ready for the birthday party and to await my arrival. I soon noticed the yawns from all of them. None of us were willing to separate, though, and we all settled down on the couch for a family nap. I'd left at an insanely early time, making my flight pretty much a red-eye. I'd leave as late in the day as possible to extend my time at home. I didn't care how tired I was when I went in the next day.

An alarm went off when it was time for us to head to the birthday celebration, which was being held at a local bounce house nearby. Evy had no energy to host one at the house. She'd arranged for Jonathan to pick up the cake, and a place would deliver the pizza and pop later.

Besides Geneva, a couple of other friends from the daycare had received invitations.

Jonathan asked me how the shooting was going for the movie. I shared what I could, though a lot of it had to be kept secret. Jonathan understood this; he was really just making small talk.

Evy and I sat side by side, watching the twins enjoy their birthday celebration. They were having a great time running and jumping with their friends.

"When do you need to leave?" Probed Evy. While she really didn't want to know, she knew she had to ask.

Leaning my head close to hers to make myself heard above the noise, I shared, "Not until bedtime. I'd then get to LA around midnight Pacific Time. What time does the party end?"

"5:30 pm. I doubt any of the kids will do much more jumping after they eat food." She hesitated. "Do you think you'll be able to come back home again before filming is done?"

Heaving a sigh, I removed my hand from hers and laced my fingers together, bracing my hands on my legs. I stared down at the floor, not wanting to look her in the eyes. "I doubt it. The producer barely gave me today off to come for this." Glancing up at her, I trailed off at the tear that was falling down one cheek. "Please don't cry. This is tearing me apart already."

Evy lifted a hand to wipe away the lonesome drop. She hadn't even realized it had leaked out. "I'm sorry. I didn't even know it was there."

"Once the party is over, we can talk more. It's a little loud here for a full conversation."

After the birthday party was over and we were back home, we continued the talk we'd started. I reassured her that while I probably couldn't come back for a scheduled visit over the remaining four weeks of the film schedule, I wouldn't hesitate to leave if a problem arose.

"You and the kids are my world," I promised, laying a hand on her cheek. We were lying in bed after I'd bathed the twins. I'd missed that ritual so much. We'd both put them to bed, but I'd been the one to read the two a bedtime story. Now Evy and I had some time to ourselves before I had to leave.

"As you and they are mine." She replied in return. "But I don't expect you to just leave your job before it's done. I have my mom, aunt, and Jonathan here if something were to happen."

I tapped the engagement ring on Evy's finger. "This here means that I'll take care of you. You, Matthew, and Cora. You're my family. By putting this ring on your hand, I promised to be there for you all, no matter what. I will stand by that." I picked up her hand and kissed the pearl on the ring.

Pushing her head back down onto my shoulder, I encouraged her to go to sleep. I'd leave when I needed to, but promised not to wake her up. I just needed these last moments with her.

Chapter 20

I lay in bed staring at the ceiling, waiting for Henry's call. It was later than usual.

I told myself it didn't mean anything, but the longer the silence stretched, the harder it was not to think about how far away he was. Again.

I shifted, trying to get comfortable, but the ache in my back flared the moment I moved. My hips protested next; the weight of the girls making even the smallest adjustment feel like work.

"Come on," I muttered under my breath, rolling carefully onto my side.

The pillow helped. A little. Not enough.

I exhaled slowly, one hand resting on my stomach, feeling the steady pull of it. Everything felt heavier lately. Slower. Even sleep didn't come easy anymore.

And still... no call.

I'd just dozed off when my phone rang. As I reached for my phone next to me, I accidentally hung up on the call instead of answering it. I swore and tried to call Henry back immediately.

He picked up on the first ring and right away asked, "Is everything okay? Why did you hang up?"

"It was an accident. I hit the button when I grabbed my phone. Everything is fine." I explained to him, trying to allay the fear I could hear in his voice.

The relief coming over the line was almost tangible. "Thank goodness. You had me worried for a second there. How was the appointment today?"

I shared the details of everything given by the doctor earlier in the day. I told Henry about the belly support harness, and the OB said that I believed the girls would be born early, considering my previous pregnancy and the current measurements. He asked me how I'd been feeling, and I was honest with him.

"I want you to take it easy. Please have your mom, aunt, and Jonathan help you out as much as possible. I love you so much, and it's tearing me apart not to be there with you," agonized Henry.

"Henry please. I hate our talks ending up like this. I know it's hard for you being far away. It's hard for me too. But it makes it harder when we focus on the distance between us. Can we talk about other topics instead?" I pleaded with him.

Henry must've heard the beseeching tone because he agreed, and we finished by talking about the filming and how daycare was going for Matthew and Cora. He also shared with me that his brother had called and told him that his wife was due any day. Henry was sad that he couldn't go see his nephew when he was born. We discussed going to visit them and his parents after the girls arrived. However, there was an undercurrent of despair and disappointment throughout the rest of our exchange.

HENRY

No one came near me.

They didn't have to say anything. The way conversations died when I walked past, the extra space people left around my chair, told me everything I needed to know.

I watched the scene play out in front of me, jaw tight, fingers tapping against my thigh. It felt like it was dragging, every take slower than the last.

"Again," the director called.

I dragged a hand through my hair and exhaled sharply.

Evy was thirty-three weeks pregnant.

I should've been home.

I leaned forward, not taking my eyes off the set. "How many more scenes do I have?" I asked.

Erik shifted beside me, already pulling up the schedule.

Before Erik could answer, my phone rang. When I glanced down, I saw it was Evy's number. She wouldn't be calling during the day unless it was something important.

I put up a finger to Erik and answered my phone to hear Evy crying. Grasping the arm of the chair with my free hand, I leaned forward. "Evy? What's wrong?"

"It's….it's the babies," Evy said between sobs.

I stood up so fast that my chair fell backward. "Tell me what's going on."

Whirling to Erik, I covered the phone and announced. "I'm leaving the set now and heading right to the airport. Get my jet ready."

I started out of the film studio sound stage with Erik following me, trying to ask questions.

The director yelled at me to stop, but I ignored him completely and continued out the big bay doors. I went back to listening to Evy.

"I just got done with my appointment; we haven't even left the parking lot. My blood pressure is too high, and the doctor doesn't like the stats on the girls. I continue to be in pain despite using the belly support. The doctor has put me on bed rest immediately. Now I have to contact work. They haven't even hired my substitute yet, and someone needs to start tomorrow." I could hear her sobbing through the phone and kept walking through the studio lot until I got to where I'd parked my car. Erik was still behind me, trying to keep up, unaware of what was going on. I heard him on the phone talking to the airport.

"First, I need you to calm down, Evy. Take some deep breaths. Then, I want you to have the driver take you home. You don't have to go back to work today, right?" I was quickly figuring out in my head what time it was in Michigan.

I led her in taking a few breaths to calm down. While I did that, I arrived at my car and put her on speakerphone while I texted her driver,

Gladys, to take her home. I also texted Maria, Evy's bodyguard, to arrange for dinner to be delivered so that Evy wouldn't have to worry about anything.

Erik headed to the airport, knowing without being told that I wouldn't need to go back to the condo for anything. Now that I had Evy calmer, I tried to find out what needed to be done for her work.

"Can I contact work for you, or do you need to do that?" I asked her. She was still on speakerphone while I texted the director back. Erik and he would collaborate to determine the remaining schedule for the scenes. I would be gone indefinitely. The man was beyond unhappy and threatening a lawsuit. I knew there wasn't a chance of one holding up when I could file for Family Medical Leave, which I planned to have Erik do.

Giving my attention back to Evy, I heard her give a shuddering sigh. "I have to contact my HR department. The doctor gave me a letter that they'll need. There'll be no argument; it's just inconvenient. They had been procrastinating about hiring someone. Luckily, I pretty much have my sub plans done and can write some from home for the next few weeks."

Now that she had calmed down, Evy was much clearer about what needed to be done. That made me feel better, but I was still going home. I couldn't leave the handling of her bed rest and my family being taken care of to others.

I continued to talk to her until I was sure she was calm and I was almost at the airport. Once there, I told her I had to go, but not why. I didn't want to tell her I was on the way and upset her by letting her know I was leaving the set.

In the air, I connected my phone to the airplane's Wi-Fi and called the film's director. I needed to take care of that before I landed.

"Hello, Jack. Before you start into me, I had to leave," I began the conversation.

"What the hell do you mean you HAD to leave?!" The older man bellowed into the line. I'd worked with the director on all the Vigil Warden films, but that didn't mean I was going to get special treatment.

I had to hold the phone away from my ear, and when that didn't work, I put the call on speakerphone and set it on the armrest next to me. "Jack… Jack… Jack." I said the man's name three times, but when that didn't break through his tirade, I let him just go on.

"You're the star of the film. You can't just walk off the set! I should fire you! Break your contract, find you in breach, and make you pay a ton of fines!" The threats continued on and on.

When there was a pause, I butted in quickly. "The babies are in distress, and Evy got put on bed rest, Jack."

I knew as soon as the director comprehended what I'd said. Jack had three kids of his own, now all adults, and five grandchildren.

"I'll have Erik file the paperwork for FMLA. He'll also work with your team to set up a day when I will return to shoot the remaining scenes that need me in them. I hope you can now understand why I left." The pleading was clear in my voice.

A sigh came over the line. "File that paperwork ASAP. Otherwise, everyone else is going to be on my butt, and there will be nothing I can do. With only ten days left of filming, this won't look good, no matter the reason. I get it, I really do, but your contract is legally binding. Don't make me sic legal on you, Ace. Take care of your family, but do it the right way."

With that, Jack hung up. I let my head fall back. It hadn't been an easy call, but the result was what I'd hoped for.

EVY

I lay on my side on the bed. I'd also been on bed rest with Matthew and Cora. It had been the worst experience of my life, and with them it had only been a little over a week. I was just thirty-four weeks into this pregnancy, and the doctor wanted me to get to at least thirty-six weeks, but preferably thirty-seven weeks. That was how far I'd made it with my first pregnancy.

The difference was that I hadn't been taking care of two preschoolers before while also working. My mom and aunt had been over every evening to help make dinner, and Jonathan had been doing my grocery shopping. But I still had to get up every morning to get the twins and myself ready.

I jumped when the door to the house crashed open. As I pushed myself up, I'd barely turned to the bedroom door when Henry enveloped me in his arms. The safety and relief I felt were immediate, and I hugged him with all I had before pulling back.

"Wait? Why are you here? Are you done with shooting?" I speculated.

"I rushed here as soon as you called me. Filming be damned." answered Henry. "You and the girls are my first and only priority."

I lay back down against the mound of pillows on the bed. I still hadn't wrapped my head around the fact that he was here. "How does that work with your contract? Can they say you're in breach?"

"Erik is filing Family Medical Leave for me as we speak, if he hasn't already. They can't sue me for breach. I'm also willing to fulfill my contract, just at a later date and with an adjusted timeline. Everything will work out." Henry leaned over to kiss me on the forehead. "Now, when do I need to go pick up the munchkins?"

Chapter 21

HENRY

I walked through the new house with the builder. It was the day after I'd arrived back, and I'd come over to do this right after dropping off the twins at daycare. I wanted — no, needed — the house done as soon as possible, especially with Evy on bedrest and the strong possibility of the girls being born early. Our little home could handle bringing them there if needed, but it would be ideal if our larger home could be ready.

Next, I had plans to meet with the interior designer and check on the progress with her. I'd been texting periodically with her as questions came up, but again, with the schedule for things being moved up, purchasing furniture, appliances, etc., would need to happen quickly. By the time I was done with the walk-through and then the meeting with the designer, it was almost time to pick up Matthew and Cora from daycare. I'd hoped to spend time with Evy and had texted her an apology for being away.

When I arrived home, my next chore was to work on dinner. I was ready to prove that I could take care of my family. Before taking the twins to daycare that morning, I'd looked through the fridge and cabinets, happy to see that someone had filled them, most likely Jonathan. I'd heard that Evy's best friend had been helping with the grocery shopping. I would need to remember to do something as a thank you. It helped to find plenty of ingredients to choose from to make a meal.

I'd just started making pasta and finished defrosting chicken for dinner when I heard Evy call out to me. When the twins and I had arrived home, she'd been napping, so I'd warned the two children to keep it quiet.

Putting the flame under the pasta pot on low and setting the chicken aside, I left the kitchen and went to the bedroom. I found Evy trying to push herself upright. Rushing over, I helped her with the pillows so that she was comfortable.

"Can I get you anything? I just started dinner and I'm making chicken alfredo with broccoli." I told her.

Shaking her water bottle at me to show it was empty, she replied. "More water, please?"

"Coming right up!" I took the bottle from her with a smile and headed right off to fill it.

While in the kitchen filling her water bottle, I checked on the pasta, twisted the dial back up to boil, cut the chicken, and set it to cook. I returned with the full bottle of water and handed it to Evy, who immediately drank quite a bit of it.

"How are you feeling? Dinner should be ready in about half an hour."

Evy instantly replied. "Bored. Tired. Sick of these four walls already."

Chuckling, I ran a hand through her hair. "I can only imagine. After dinner, I'll update you on the house. I've got a bunch of questions to ask you, and we can look through catalogs to pick out stuff we need. Maybe that'll take your mind off things. I have to get back to dinner now. Can I get you anything else before I head to the kitchen?"

"No, I'm fine for now. Don't mind me. I'm just mopey."

Kissing her on the forehead, I went to finish dinner. When it was done, I set two portions aside so I could eat with her in the bedroom after I fed the twins. I called Matthew and Cora into the kitchen to eat, then cleaned up their dishes and put away the leftovers.

While I ate dinner with Evy, we discussed names for the girls, as that was something we hadn't done yet. Evy had actually done some thinking on this while I'd been out of town. She shared the ones she had contemplated with me.

"I still had a list of names from when I had the twins. I had quite a few girl names on it and still like a lot of them. Grace, Rose, Hannah, Penelope, Sadie, and Ruby are some of them." Evy read off the names from a notebook that she had removed from her bedside stand.

I frowned and shook my head when she got to Sadie. "I worked with a Sadie on a movie once. Bad vibes there."

Evy laughed at that. "Okay, fine, no Sadie."

Leaning back on one elbow, I rubbed my jaw with one finger and my thumb while weighing the other names. "I kind of like how Grace and Rose go together. As one name. I also like Hannah, but I'm not sure I like any of the other names for a middle name."

"Well, three out of four names picked that quickly is quite a feat. I think we can figure out a middle name over the next couple of weeks. Now, let's look at picking out the nursery items for our Grace and Hannah." Evy reached for the laptop that I'd brought in, ready to design the room for our baby girls.

While I hated to do it, I had to leave and fly to Los Angeles for two days. Erik had put in a lot of time and effort to arrange that I would only need to go back for just one day of filming to finish some scenes.

I'd arranged for Maeve to stay at the house for the entire time I was gone. I'd even precooked meals, so she didn't have to do that, trying to make it as easy as possible. Jonathan was on call as the backup person just in case anything were to happen.

I insisted on the earlier flight.

"Day before," I'd said on the phone, already halfway through packing the few things I'd need. "I'll get in, sleep, adjust, and be ready to go."

Evy had been quiet for a second. "You're really doing a one-day turnaround?"

"A little over, technically," I corrected. "But yeah. I don't want to be gone longer than I have to."

"You could stay an extra night," she offered gently. "Make it easier on yourself."

"I'll sleep better at home," I said without hesitation.

"...with me," she said.

"Yeah," I admitted. "With you."

The condo felt wrong the second I walked in. Too quiet. Too still. I glanced around as if something might've changed in my absence. It hadn't. Everything was exactly as I'd left it. Clean, minimal, untouched. I exhaled and ran a hand through my hair.

Later that night, I lay in bed, staring at the ceiling. No soft rustle of blankets. No quiet shift beside me. No steady, familiar rhythm of Evy's breathing. I turned onto my side, then onto my back again.

"Great," I muttered under my breath. After another few minutes, I grabbed my phone and hit her name.

She answered on the second ring. "Hey."

"You're still up?" I asked. While it was midnight in Los Angeles, it was 3:00 am in Michigan.

"Yeah," she said. "I couldn't sleep."

I swallowed a quiet laugh. "Same."

"Jet lag already?" she teased lightly.

"No," I said. "It's just... too quiet here."

There was a soft pause. "I can leave the phone on," she offered. "If you want."

I hesitated, then gave in. "Yeah. I want."

"Okay," she breathed.

A faint rustle sounded on her end, then the quiet, familiar rhythm of her breathing filled the line. I closed my eyes.

"Better?" she murmured.

"Yeah," I said, voice low. "Much."

"Go to sleep," she whispered.

"You too."

"Goodnight, Henry."

"Night, Evy."

I didn't remember when I fell asleep, but I did.

The next morning came early. Too early. I walked onto the soundstage with coffee in hand, already dressed, already focused.

"Look who decided to show up," a crew member called.

"Alright, places!" the director called.

I stepped into position, the set lights warming around me.

"Ready?" another actor asked quietly.

I nodded once. "Let's go."

The first scene rolled, and just like that, I was in it. Focused. Precise. Controlled.

"Cut!"

"Good. Reset."

We moved fast. Scene after scene. Dialogue, movement, emotion — I hit every mark without hesitation.

By midday, the director was already impressed. "Whatever you did to prep," he said, watching the playback, "keep doing it."

I took a sip of water. "Noted."

"Next setup in five!"

By early evening, we were wrapping my final scene.

"And... cut!" the director called. "That's a wrap for Ace."

A few scattered claps broke out across the set. I nodded in thanks, already stepping back, already mentally moving on. Heading to the car, I didn't even bother pretending to hide how I felt. I pulled out my phone and dialed Evy. Erik pulled out of the parking lot and headed towards the airport at the same time.

She answered almost immediately. "Hey."

"I'm done," I said.

"That was fast."

"Told you I'd get it all done."

There was a smile in her voice. "Proud of you."

I leaned back against the seat, letting out a breath. "Flight's being readied."

"Of course it is."

"I'll be home late."

A small pause. "I like the sound of that," she said.

"Yeah," I replied. "Me too."

"Get some rest," she added. "You deserve it."

I smiled faintly, already thinking about being home.

Chapter 22

HENRY

Driving to the doctor's office, I held Evy's hand. Today was the thirty-six week checkup and ultrasound. Evy had been having pretty strong Braxton Hicks contractions all weekend. We were both eager and anxious to hear what the doctor had to say. After the appointment, I was meeting with the builder to do the final walkthrough of the house and permit check.

During the measurement-taking, Evy saw my face take on a look of unease. I tried to hide it, but it made her uneasy as well. She could tell that the doctor was spending more time than usual doing some checks. Before she turned them over to the ultrasound tech for the ultrasound, the doctor reviewed her findings.

"Well, you are 2 cm dilated and 30% effaced. Don't get too excited. There are women who stay that way for weeks. But I want you to really take it easy. You've been staying in bed completely, right?" The doctor didn't look at Evy but at me instead when she asked the question.

I answered at once. "Of course. The only times she gets up are to use the bathroom or shower. I serve her all meals in bed."

"Good. That's what I want to continue. I'd really like to see these babies stay in that womb for as long as possible."

Two days later, I awoke to the sound of Evy crying out and her nails digging into my arm. In a moment she let go, but I knew I had indentations from it. I reached out and switched on the bedside lamp, then rolled over and looked at her. It took me just a second to figure out what was going on.

"You're in labor, aren't you?" I guessed, seeing the sweat on her brow and the pain in her eyes.

"What gave you the first clue, Sherlock?" Her snide reply was all I needed to confirm my suspicion.

Jumping out of bed, I put on the nearest pants, shirt, and shoes I could find. We had already packed a hospital bag as soon as we'd returned from the doctor's appointment the other day. I grabbed that along with my phone and called Maeve's number.

"Maeve? Evy's in labor; I need you to come over and stay with Matthew and Cora." As I made the call, I took the bag out to the SUV. One of the night security guards gave me a look as I did so. I motioned for the man to wait a moment.

"I'll be right over." Maeve only said that one sentence and then hung up.

Waving the security guard over, I said to him, "I need you to be the driver tonight. Evy is in labor." I didn't wait for a reply and headed back inside just as Maeve arrived to join me.

I came back helping Evy walk, and the guard helped place her in the vehicle. We raced off to the hospital, and I called on the way to let them know when we'd arrive. I didn't even notice the couple of paparazzi vehicles that followed us.

Thankfully, the hospital wasn't far away.

Evy

The labor was shorter than I expected.

One moment everything was tightening and building, and then it was over. Two cries, one after the other, filled the room and stole every breath I had left.

I didn't realize I was crying until Henry brushed his thumb across my cheek.

"They're here," he breathed.

Grace Rose came first, small and perfect in a way that didn't seem possible. Hannah Jade followed close behind, just as tiny, just as strong.

"They're both doing great," the doctor said, moving between them with practiced calm. "And your blood pressure is already coming down."

I let out a shaky breath.

The tightness that had been wrapped around my body for weeks eased, little by little. The ache in my back dulled. The constant pressure that had followed me through every hour of the day began to lift.

"Everything looks good," the doctor added. "You did exactly what you needed to do."

That was all I needed to hear.

I sank back into the pillow, exhausted but lighter than I had been in months.

"They're beautiful," Henry whispered.

I turned my head toward him, then back to the girls, still trying to take it all in.

We were all okay.

The first afternoon, my mom and Aunt Eileen had brought Matthew and Cora up to see their sisters. The hospital room door opened softly.

Mom peeked in first, smiling. "Alright... are we ready?"

I shifted slightly in the bed, glancing at Henry. "I think so."

Henry nodded, a grin already forming. "Yeah. Bring them in."

Mom stepped aside. "Okay, you two, quiet voices."

Matthew and Cora walked in slowly, their usual energy dialed down to something almost reverent.

"Whoa..." Matthew whispered.

Cora clutched her Great-Aunt Eileen's hand. "Tiny..."

Henry stepped closer to them, crouching slightly. "Want to come see?"

They nodded immediately. I carefully adjusted the blankets so they could see both babies. "These are your sisters," I said softly.

Matthew leaned in, eyes wide. "Sisters?"

Henry chuckled quietly. "Yes, we're outnumbered now."

Cora tilted her head, studying them. "So little?"

"They're brand new," I said with a gentle smile.

Matthew pointed carefully. "That one moved!"

I laughed softly. "That's Grace."

Cora's voice dropped to a whisper. "Can they hear us?"

"Yes, you can talk to them," Henry said.

Cora leaned in just a little closer. "Hi, babies," she whispered.

Matthew looked up at Henry. "I hold one?"

Henry glanced at me.

I smiled. "We'll try later, with help."

Matthew nodded seriously. "Okay."

Cora reached out, then hesitated. "Can I touch?"

I guided her gently. "Just very soft."

Cora's finger brushed lightly against the baby's hand.

She gasped. "She grabbed me!"

Henry smiled, watching her. "Yeah. That's Hannah."

Matthew shook his head, still staring. "So cool."

Now Gramma to four, my mom wiped at her eyes quietly. "It really is."

Aunt Eileen smiled warmly. "You've got a full house now."

Henry glanced at me, something deeper in his expression. "Yeah, we do."

Miriam and John were flown in to see their new granddaughters and immediately came up to the hospital. Henry's brother, wife, and the baby had decided to wait to visit once they were home. Later that evening, the door opened again — this time with far less hesitation.

"Miriam, slow down," John said, though he was smiling just as much.

"I've waited all day," Miriam shot back, already stepping inside.

Henry stood immediately. "Mom."

She barely paused before pulling him into a quick hug. "You did good," she murmured.

John clapped Henry on the shoulder. "Congratulations, son."

"Thanks," Henry said, a little softer now.

Miriam moved toward the bed, her expression shifting the moment she saw the babies.

"Oh..." she breathed. "Oh, they're beautiful."

I smiled, tired but glowing. "Hi."

Miriam looked up. "Hi, sweetheart." Her voice softened even more. "How are you feeling?"

"Tired," I admitted. "But good."

"You look amazing," Miriam said, clearly meaning it.

John stepped closer, peering down. "Two of them," he said, a hint of awe in his voice. "That's something."

Henry smirked lightly. "Yeah. We didn't do anything halfway."

John chuckled. "Clearly."

Miriam reached out carefully. "Can I?"

I nodded. "Of course."

Miriam gently lifted one of the babies, her entire demeanor shifting as she held her.

"Oh, look at you..." she whispered. "Hello, little one."

Henry told his mom, "You're holding Hannah. Grace is still in the bassinet."

John leaned closer. "She's got a strong grip already."

Everyone laughed softly.

Miriam glanced between the two babies, then back at me. "You've given us quite the gift."

My smile softened. "They're pretty special."

Henry stepped closer to me, his hand brushing lightly against mine. "Yeah," he said quietly. "They are."

Henry glanced around the room, at me, the babies, his parents, and shook his head slightly, smiling.

So far, nursing both girls had been going well. Since this was my second set of twins, I had the advantage of knowing how to nurse twins. I'd impressed the nurses with how I handled both babies at once. Henry had more of a learning curve, not having really any experience with babies. Just picking up and holding either of the girls was still terrifying for him. They were so tiny and seemed fragile.

"I've never seen someone do that so smoothly," one of them had said, arms crossed as she leaned against the counter.

I'd shrugged lightly. "Practice."

Henry, on the other hand, had stood off to the side, equal parts impressed and overwhelmed.

"I don't even know where to look," he admitted quietly.

"Start with their heads," I teased. "That's usually a good place."

He huffed a soft laugh, though his eyes stayed glued to the girls. "They're so small."

"They are," I said gently. "But they're stronger than they look."

He wasn't convinced. Even just picking them up had been a process.

"Okay, so I just... lift?" he asked one morning, hovering his hands uncertainly over Grace.

"Yes," I said, trying not to smile. "But support her head."

"I am supporting her head," he insisted.

"Henry, that's her shoulder."

He froze. "That feels like a design flaw."

I laughed. "You'll get it."

"I'd like a manual," he muttered, carefully adjusting his grip.

By the time we were ready to go home, though, Henry had become an expert at diaper changes and swaddling. His next challenge was the infant car seat. He watched me put Grace in hers, then he took on Hannah's. I'd made it look so easy, then laughed at him when he botched it. I had come to the rescue of his poor daughter before he wrapped her up in the harness.

Before we headed home, there was one obstacle. Reporters had been camped outside the hospital since the day I'd gone into labor.

We gathered everything; the nurses offering final congratulations as we headed toward the exit. But before the doors even came into view, we heard it.

Voices. Cameras. A low, constant buzz of movement.

Henry's expression shifted immediately. "They're still here."

"Of course they are," I muttered.

A nurse hesitated. "Do you want security to escort you out?"

Henry nodded once. "Yes. Please."

As we waited, the noise grew louder—shouts bleeding through the doors.

"Ace! Over here!"

"Can we get a picture of the babies?"

"Are those your daughters?"

"Names! Can you give us names?"

I shifted slightly, instinctively drawing closer to the girls. "They're not even trying to be quiet."

"They don't care," Henry said, his voice low.

"Are we really walking out into that?" I asked.

He looked at me, steady. "You won't be alone."

A security guard approached. "We'll clear a path. Stay close to us."

Henry nodded. "Thank you."

I adjusted the blanket over Grace's car seat, making sure she was covered. "I don't want their faces out there."

"They won't be," Henry said firmly. "I mean it," he said, meeting my eyes. "We'll get through this, and then we're home."

I took a breath, nodding slowly. "Okay."

The doors opened. The noise hit instantly.

"Ace! Is this your family?"

"Can we see the babies?"

"Are those the twins?"

Flashes went off in rapid bursts, and I flinched slightly.

Henry stepped closer, one hand steady at my back. "Keep your head down. Just walk."

"I am," I said, gripping the handle of the car seat a little tighter.

"Over here!"

"Ace, just one comment!"

"No comments," he said sharply, not breaking stride.

Security moved ahead of us, creating a narrow path.

"Please step back."

"Give them space."

"Move back."

A camera flashed too close. Henry turned his head just enough. "Back up."

There was enough edge in his voice that a few actually did. We reached the SUV, and the door opened. "In," he said.

I slid in quickly, pulling the girls close as Henry climbed in right behind me. The door shut—and just like that; the noise was gone. Silence filled the car.

I looked down at the girls, both still asleep despite everything. "They slept through that."

He glanced over, a small, incredulous smile forming. "Good sign."

"Well," I said softly, "we survived the first one."

Henry reached over, his hand brushing mine. "And we'll handle the next."

I squeezed his hand gently. "Let's go home."

Since I hadn't yet really seen any of the finished new house, Henry heard me gasp at my first view of it. Even though the landscaping had yet to be done, the S-curve that led us to the front of the house was impressive.

There was a full porch that ran the length of the front, and it already had the hanging swing that we had chosen on it as well as a set of patio furniture. The SUV parked right up next to the front door. Maeve opened the door, and Eileen, Miriam, John, Matthew, and Cora all came out to welcome us. Once on the porch, Maeve took the car seat and gave me a hug. I knelt and took the twins into my arms.

As we walked through our new home, I saw how what were once just drawings was now our home. I cried seeing the girls' and twins' rooms. When I opened the door to our main suite, I stood in delight at the open space that would become our retreat from family chaos.

Henry

I watched Evy turn toward me, her arms slipping around my waist, her smile soft and full in a way I hadn't seen before.

Something in my chest settled.

I glanced past her, taking it all in. The girls. The twins. Our families filling the space around us. The house that finally felt lived in instead of imagined.

Evy leaned into me, and I wrapped my arms around her without thinking.

I didn't need anything else.

Chapter 23

HENRY

Seven Weeks Later

The town of Belding had never seen an event like this happen before. Outside the church, security was checking invitations and keeping reporters at bay.

Ivory tulle bows and purple calla lilies adorned the pews of the church at each end.

We had timed the wedding ceremony purpose-ly for the sun to shine through the twenty-foot tall windows that faced the river and reflected the light. We limited the number of people invited to the ceremony–mostly family and very close friends, with only a few A-listers or anyone related to the film industry. People considered it the event of the summer, and with fewer than 100 attendees, invitations were precious.

It had been seven and a half weeks since the girls were born. Everyone had settled into being a family of six. We'd just settled into a regular sleeping routine, for which we were both grateful. Tonight would be our first night without them. The three grandparents and great aunt were taking them and the twins for our wedding night.

In the anteroom next to the chapel, I waited anxiously for the ceremony to start. I'd gone with a suit rather than a tuxedo for the wedding. I didn't know what Evy was wearing for a wedding dress, but I knew it wasn't white or ivory. She said that as a bride for the second time; she didn't need to wear one. Those were the only details she had shared with me about it. I knew the wedding colors were ivory and deep purple, but beyond that I didn't know what to expect when I saw her coming down the aisle.

Evy

I paced in the room at the back of the chapel. I swore I hadn't felt this nervous when I'd gotten married to Vincent. The girls were finally asleep after having nursed. Matthew and Cora were running around the small room, and I was letting them so they could burn off some energy. I was also waiting to get them dressed in their outfits so they didn't ruin them. Eileen and Miriam are also in the room with me, helping to keep track of the children and to calm me down because it was obvious that my nerves were high.

I twisted the pearl engagement ring on my ring finger. I didn't know why I felt so tense today. Henry and I had been together for almost a year now. Heck, we even had two children together and had been living together. I had no cold feet about marrying him. I loved him with everything I had.

My mother came up behind me and put a hand on my shoulder. "Evy, what's wrong?"

"I don't know. I don't know why I feel nervous," I confessed.

"It's just wedding day jitters. Every bride gets them. Just take a deep breath, put that dress on and get ready to walk down that aisle." My mother smiled reassuringly at me and then gave me a hug.

Suddenly, everything felt right. I didn't know why that little pep talk from my mom changed everything, but it did. I gave my mom a gigantic hug back and then spun to the gown hanging next to me. We'd found it at a bridal store in a nearby town and knew it was my dress upon first glance. It was a strapless gown with a shirred top, a sweetheart neckline, and a full A-line bottom. The colors were what set it off. It was an abstract blend of purple, magenta, white, and navy. Definitely not a traditional bridal gown, but that hadn't been what I'd wanted.

Matthew would wear a suit that matched Henry's with a purple tie to match the color theme. Cora's dress was a purple, sleeveless satin with a sash that was the same shade as Matthew's tie. It had been harder to find the same color purple for the babies' dresses, with them being so little. Theirs were half satin, half soft tulle with matching headbands and diaper covers in a purple that was just a shade different from their sibling's.

My mom helped me put on my dress first. We'd been to the salon before coming to the church. The stylist had curled my hair into ringlets and then pinned it into an updo.

After I was ready, the grandmothers dressed the four children. Cora looked grown-up in her little ball gown, and Matthew like Vincent in his suit. Vincent had declined his invitation to the wedding, though he had sent a card. Finally, everyone was ready, and it was almost time for the ceremony.

HENRY

I stood at the front of the chapel, waiting. Everyone was sitting and music was playing. I watched as Cora walked down the church aisle carrying her small bouquet. She looked so pretty in her purple satin dress. Matthew came next in a smaller version of my own suit. He carried a small pillow with our wedding bands tied to it. The boy was taking his job seriously, watching where he placed his feet to make sure he didn't lose the rings, which he wouldn't.

Evy's mom carried Hannah, and my mom carried Grace down the aisle behind Matthew. My two daughters were sleeping and looked like angels. Most would probably believe it, but I knew that when they were hungry, tired, or grumpy, they could scream like demons.

The music changed to the bridal march, and I switched my gaze to the back of the chapel. Evy appeared on my father's arm. Since her father had passed away, she decided John would walk her down the aisle.

I had to clench my jaw to physically stop it from dropping upon seeing her. Not in shock but in awe. What I saw was the most beautiful sight ever walking towards me.

The dress fit her well, and few would guess that she had just given birth to twins not quite eight weeks ago. She had trimmed back down fairly quickly. People said that nursing was the quickest way to shed baby weight, and Evy was proof of that. The dress was like none I'd ever seen on a bride, but the style and color fit my bride perfectly. She held a bouquet of ivory calla lilies with sprigs of lavender tied with a deep purple ribbon.

I watched her walk towards me as if it were a dream. Soon she stood in front of me, and my own father placed her hand in mine. I barely heard the priest say the vows, but I must've responded in the correct places with the right words because the next thing I was aware of was hearing, "Please place the ring on her finger."

I looked down to see the priest hand me the wedding band that Evy and I had picked out together. She was holding it out to place it on my left hand, which I still had at my side. I lifted it so she could slide the ring on. I then did the same to her, nestling the band up against the black pearl engagement ring I'd placed there only a few months ago.

The priest then covered both our hands with his, proclaimed us married, and said a blessing. I then stepped forward to kiss my bride. Leaning in, I wrapped my arms around Evy, drew her close, and pressed my lips to hers. I heard her gasp as I deepened it, despite the crowd watching us. Tipping her backward, I continued the kiss as hoots and hollers filled the church.

Ending the kiss, I brought Evy back up and saw she had a blush and a huge smile on her face. I smiled back at her, thrilled to realize that I was her husband now. We turned together to the people who joined us for our wedding and raised our joined hands before walking down the aisle.

Greeting our guests after the ceremony and then the reception was mostly a blur. Key moments that stuck in my head were the toasts, the cutting of the cake, my first dance with Evy, and dancing with Cora. Later, the many photos taken by the photographer and others at the reception would help me recall all the other details that made it such a wonderful night.

EVY

Upon entering our hotel suite, the first thing I did was kick off my heeled sandals. While they were wedges and not stilettos or thin heels, they still were killing my feet. I then walked over to the bed and fell back onto it, closing my eyes as I did so. As I landed, I heard Henry laugh at me.

Henry. My husband. That sounded so nice. It made me grin.

"What are you smiling about?" I opened my eyes to see him looming over me. He braced his hands to hold himself up with his arms straight. I stayed lying straight on the bed as he picked up one hand to move a piece of hair from my face that had fallen from my updo.

I swallowed, not willing to tell him exactly what I'd been thinking. "Nothing much, just happy that you're my husband."

"And I'm happy you're my wife." He countered back. "Now, wife, I think it's time to get you out of that dress, however much it looks good on you. How about a shower before bed?"

I nodded and let Henry help me up. He twisted me around to unzip the dress, and it fell to the floor, leaving me in only a pair of pale pink lace bikini panties. The dress had had cups sewn into it, so I hadn't needed to wear a bra. I heard him suck in his breath once he saw how little I now had on, or really didn't have on. His hands reached around to cup my breasts, which were still larger than previously from nursing the girls. I'd taken a break during the reception to nurse them and would need to pump later.

My nipples were sensitive and reacted to his touch. My head fell back against his shoulder as he squeezed, tweaked, and caressed them. The doctor had given me permission for 'intimate relations' last week during my six-week post-natal checkup. I'd had to do physical therapy twice a week for three weeks for some pelvic muscle rehabilitation from carrying the girls, but I'd finished that up three days ago. We'd partially planned our wedding date around that.

I breathed out a word that Henry must not have caught at first. Then I said it again. "Shower."

He spun me in his arms, lifted me up, and carried me bridal-style to the bathroom. Setting me down, he turned on the shower to warm up, and then faced me. I ran my hands up his chest, under the suit jacket to his shoulders, and then pushed it up then down his arms. Before it fell to the floor, I'd already moved to the buttons of his shirt, slowly sliding each one open, my tongue licking my lips as his skin appeared to my view. Apparently too slowly for Henry's liking, as he opened the ones at the bottom, hurrying the process. When I tried to stop him, he groaned and took my hands in his, drawing them behind my back.

I was suddenly being held captive by one hand as he undid his belt and then pants with the other. He dropped these to the floor and then moved both of us into the shower spray, both of us clad in our underwear.

The water drenched us, and the fabric left soon revealed everything. Henry pressed me against the shower wall, then tugged off and tossed aside my panties. I did the same to Henry's soaking wet briefs.

Henry then sank to his knees as he kissed his way down my body to my center. Stopping at my stomach, he took his time to worship this area. It was not flat after carrying the girls, but he didn't care. The additional stretch marks were just signs that I'd carried his children, and he loved me more for that. He put one leg over his shoulder as he pressed his mouth to my core. I put my fist to my mouth as he licked, kissed, and teased me. I quickly climaxed, and Henry kept me from falling.

He stood and wiped his mouth with the back of his hand while trying not to smirk at my dazed expression. When I reached for him, he shook his head and instead helped me to wash my hair first, then my body before doing the same himself.

I was still recovering when we dried off and moved to the bedroom to finish what we'd started in the shower. Henry dropped his towel to the floor next to the bed and unwound the one from around me. I decided that this was my chance to take control and be more assertive.

I started by kissing his neck, then his chest before going back to his mouth. My hands gripped his backside, and then one moved around to the front. Henry moaned into my mouth, realizing that I was taking control.

I broke off the kiss and drug my mouth down his chest to one of his nipples, lightly biting, causing him to hiss. Smiling to myself at his response, I continued on to my goal. I wanted to do to him what he had done to me in the shower. Henry's hand was soon wrapped in my hair as I took him into my mouth.

It wasn't long, though, before Henry was reaching down and drawing me upward. "That's enough. I need you now. On the bed." He commanded.

We weren't shy with each other and didn't have expectations for our wedding night. Which meant that when Henry put me on the bed on my stomach, but then raised my hips in the air to enter me from behind, I didn't protest. In fact, I peered at him out of the corner of my eye to watch as he ran his hand over my rump before sliding himself home. I sobbed with the feeling of being filled with him again.

I pushed myself up further on my knees to change the angle. Doing so caused Henry to mutter my name and grasp my hips harder. His pace increased, and I reached down to rub myself in the place where I was the most sensitive.

Feeling the tightening in my center, I warned Henry, "I'm coming, I'm there!"

Henry's movements became even more frenzied as he followed me into ecstasy. He dragged me to him as he finished along with me.

Once his breathing had slowed a bit, Henry let go of me and rolled us onto our sides to lie on the bed. I felt him loosen the sheets that were under us and then wrench over to cover both of us. He kissed the top of my head and tucked it into the crook of his shoulder, letting me use it as a pillow.

"Sleep, sweetheart." Henry murmured softly. "We have the rest of our lives together from now on."

Epilogue

ACE/HENRY

Just Over One Year Later

Cameras were at the ready to take photos of the family who were stepping out of the limousine. We rarely appeared in public, so all the paparazzi wanted was the chance to capture the photo of the night.

It was the premiere of the newest and last Vigil Warden movie, *Oathbound*. After announcing that this movie would end the series, presales skyrocketed. It was occurring over the coveted Fourth of July weekend. The organizers spared no expense for the red carpet event.

The driver opened the limousine door, and everyone held their breath to see who would step out first. One black leather shoe, then another, hit the pavement, followed by the rest of me, Ace Starling, the Vigil Warden star himself, clad in a charcoal suit with a black button-up shirt under it, open at the neck. The relaxed style wasn't typical of me.

I reached a hand back into the car to help a five-year-old little girl with straight brown hair dressed in a dark lavender dress where the skirt was tulle with embroidered flowers on it. Next was a young boy, the same age as the girl, dressed in a smaller version of the tux that I was wearing. The two children stood to the side, waiting patiently.

I rotated back to the car and reached in again. This time I came out with a toddler dressed in a smaller version of the dark lavender dress worn by the other girl. Her hair was black ringlets tied up in a bow the same color as her dress. I moved her onto my hip and then reached back in to help a woman. She wore a dark lavender dress with a V-neck where the fabric criss-crossed across the front, but also had a sash at the waist that fell in a drape like a waterfall to the floor. A jewel clip held back her auburn hair on one side. She reached back into the limousine to bring out one more child. This toddler looked very similar to the other that I was still holding on my hip, except she had auburn ringlets.

I took the woman's left hand, which was adorned with a solitaire black pearl ring and a wedding band. The older children each stood on either side of their parents, holding out an arm that supported a toddler, to walk the red carpet as if they had done so a million times before. In fact, it was their first.

The fairy tale of us, the Starling couple, had made the news last year following our wedding. Film studios, authors, and journalists were still trying to buy the rights to our epic love story to turn it into a Hollywood movie, book, or feature article. We had resisted all efforts so far.

Everyone watched as we strolled down the carpeted walkway. There were murmurs about how beautiful the mother was, how well-behaved the children were, and how happy the famous actor looked. No one could deny the love that was witnessed in the looks shared between my wife and me.

When we reached the photo op area, we paused, taking time to rearrange the children for a few different shots: as we'd walked down the runway, with the toddlers standing, and letting the older children hold the younger children by the hand briefly so the two of us were alone.

Every reporter crowded in, trying to get the shot that would be on the cover of their magazine. No one knew when the next time we, as a family, would be out all together. Soon we continued on to the interview area, but only I, the star of the show, stayed there for a question and answer, and my family continued on.

Those reporters with questions crowded forward. They flew at me at a rapid rate.

"Why won't there be another Vigil Warden movie?"

"I heard a rumor of a TV series based on the movies. Any confirmation? Will you be starring in it?"

"Will there be any spin-offs?"

"What's next for you? There have been rumors you are retiring from acting."

"What was it like to say goodbye to Vigil Warden after all this time?"

"How do you move on from a role that has defined you for so long?"

"After playing Vigil Warden for six movies, what will you miss most about him?"

"What do you want to say to Vigil Warden fans?"

I listened to all the questions but gave a speech instead.

"Thank you all for your questions. There are way too many to answer, though." There was a laugh from the reporters at this. "I'm not retiring from acting but am taking a hiatus to spend time with my family and be more particular with the acting jobs I decide to take on. Family is the most important thing in life."

I paused at this and looked across the sea of faces in front of me. "Playing Vigil Warden and filming the six movies that followed that wondrous character has been an amazing experi-ence. I can never forget the people and fans that supported me in the role that helped me grow as an actor and a public media figure."

Now, not just the attention of the reporters, but practically everyone at the premiere was on me.

"Right now, I want to thank my wife for all her support and love. Without her, I would be noth-ing, and she is my everything. My children are also my reason for being here. They keep me grounded."

I took one last breath before finishing.

"Thank you again for your love of the Vigil War-den films. I hope you enjoy this last one."

I stepped away from the interview area to join my family in the cocktail room. When I walked in, I searched until I saw my wife. Walking up behind her, I reached around for a glass of champagne and nuzzled her neck.

"I hope that's my husband and not some ran-dom stranger." She mused laughingly.

"You better hope so, too!" I mockingly replied as she twisted in my arms. Looking around, I questioned. "Where are our children?"

Pointing to an area to the left of where we were, my wife grinned and revealed. "Did you know the director actually planned for a children's area tonight? And hired professional nannies? You'd think he was trying to get on your good side." She said the last with a wink.

"Seems like the old man learned something after I left the film set last year. He's definitely earning brownie points with the lead actor. Should we go check on our munchkins?" Finishing the champagne, I set the glass down on the table behind my wife.

"How long did you plan on staying? Originally, you didn't want to stay for the movie showing, right? I know the girls won't behave for much longer. They're going to get tired soon, and then we'll have some hellions on our hands." My wife crossed her arms over her chest and raised an eyebrow.

Jokingly, I questioned, "Hellions? Our two little angels?"

The bombshell next to me raised an eyebrow and challenged me. "Are you forgetting how long it took to get those two little angels dressed for this shindig? I think I remember a specific man asking whose idea it was to take two toddlers to a film premiere to begin with."

"I don't recall anything of the sort," I said with a laugh, remembering exactly what she was talking about. We'd each had to tackle a twin to get them into the cute little lavender creations.

However, knowing she was right, I figured I should talk to those I needed to quickly and then say goodbye. Taking her arm, I tucked it into my elbow. "If I need to schmooze, you're coming with me."

Laughing, my wife tossed her hair over her shoulder and let me lead her away from the food table where she had been waiting for me. I raised the hand I'd taken up to my mouth to kiss it. This is what I'd needed, wanted, craved when I'd first met her so many months ago. The reason I'd thrown caution to the wind and taken that chance.

About the Author

JS Williams writes contemporary, historical, and paranormal romance, blending emotional depth with unforgettable characters. Her debut novel, *Bride of Wolffang*, was published in July 2025.

A lifelong Michigander, JS grew up on the Sunrise Side and now lives in Grand Rapids, Michigan, with her husband and their two teenage sons. When she's not writing, she works as a school occupational therapist, supporting students in special education—a career she has devoted more than twenty-five years to.

JS is passionate about making reading accessible. She incorporates dyslexia-friendly fonts, thoughtful spacing, and visual elements into her books to support readers of all abilities.

When she isn't immersed in storytelling, you'll find her reading, traveling, working on projects for her LLC, or spending time with family and friends. A tattooed, introverted Gen Xer with a love for 80s music, JS brings both heart and authenticity to every story she tells.